BACK TO THE WINE JUG

A COMIC NOVEL IN VERSE

JOE TAYLOR

Sagging Meniscus

© 2020 by Joe Taylor

Printed in the United States of America.
Set in Williams Caslon Text with LaTeX.

ISBN: 978-1-944697-97-6 (paperback)
Library of Congress Control Number: 2020932185

Sagging Meniscus Press
Montclair, New Jersey
saggingmeniscus.com

For Sarah Langcuster, Christin Loehr, Ed Snodgrass, and Tricia Taylor, whose suggestions were invaluable.

And for Jacob Smullyan, something of a true believer.

"When I was very young I forgot in the cave of Trophonius how to laugh; when I became older, when I opened my eyes and saw reality, I started to laugh and haven't stopped since."

Søren Kierkegaard, Either/Or
trans. Alastair Hannay

CONTENTS

BACK TO THE WINE JUG

Cast of the Players and places, in order of appearance

Thalia, the Greek muse of pastoral rhyme and comedy. Much needed in our time.

Union of Poets, such serious folk, chirping words of petite woe, they lend laughter no time. Such is their stance.

Hades, the underworld. Did you really think you'd go elsewhere?

Diogenes, ancient Greek cynic, baiter of Plato. In Greece, he slept nightly in a wine jug, kept companion to dogs, masturbated in public to protest complacency, and importantly, carried a pre-Coleman lantern in eternal search of one honest (wo)man.

Victoria Woodhull, hardy nineteenth century feminist who ran for President of the United States, proponent of free love, victim of her era and her family. In her lifetime she constantly mistook manifestations of the above-mentioned Diogenes for Demosthenes (another Greek, who was an orator, whom she mistakenly viewed as her spiritual counselor). In this incarnation, Diogenes at last (and at least) is able to correct her blunder.

Lord Hades, the all-powerful lord of the underworld, where all mortal souls must go, regardless of merit or demerit. His sole response to human petitions, questions, and sadly moaning pleas? "Pshaw!"

Birmingham, a city in Alabama. Did you really think you'd go elsewhere?

Detective Alonzo Rankin, an undercover Birmingham cop. Will Diogenes' lantern ever glow upon his Creole skin?

Patrolman Smith, God-fearing and sure of himself. How sure? Too sure.

Pluto, Diogenes' favorite dog, a red Doberman revealing moments of brilliance.

The Three Ravens, aka The Three Corbies, soaring high and flying acrobatically low, they scavenge, but never judge.

J. Edgar Hoover, (in)famous Director of the F.B.I. Commies buzz forever in his ego-filled bonnet. He hates 'em and Civil Rights demonstrators, but on the saving grace side he's a lover of dogs, antiques, violet toenails, and maybe males? In this incarnation, will he discover that Marx is defunct?

Judge Roy Bean Too, infinitely better than the original, this judge has forsaken whiskey to imbibe Jesus and fourteen-year-old girls, who toot his love buzz.

Doctor Eddie Truelove, chair, UAB department of neuroscience, whose spacious car holds an infinity of necessities.

Abby, the lead Fury, themselves young women enlisted by Victoria to forward love, love, and more love. They follow Victoria with a will.

Homeless Lena, a bright and too empathetic bag lady of Birmingham who loves cats above all else. Durp.

Hot Dog Rita, an opportunist daring anywhere or anytime to sell a (hot) dog.

Slam Sam, an angry young woman, following her anger with a will.

Vulcan, assistant to Lord Hades, imbiber of red wine. AKA, **Thor.**

Joseph, step-dad to the one and only Jesus and understudy to the above.

Mary, a young sculptress "like the mother of Jesus," peacemaker, and enunciator of grand "biblical" verse. Will Diogenes' lantern ever glow upon her?

Invocation unto Thalia, Comedy's Step-slut Muse

Wherein the author laments the pallid attention his previous comic tome in rhyming verse, Pineapple, *received. He petitions Comedy's lithe muse, Thalia, who responds tersely, as befits a lithe muse.*

Austere and sublime, the Union of Poets made muster.
"Hang him!" yelled some. "Shoot him!" cried others.
(They had nor rope nor gun to back their bluster.)
His crime that angered such fine sisters and brothers?

Defaming poesy's tongue to crack slim jokes,
ignoring their low tragic. Impolitic, puerile,
he'd used honeyed meter, sweet rhyme to stoke
their pimple moans high, ignite views worthwhile,

attain a laugh just now and then. Such was his style.
And such they abhorred, for poesy—you surely know—
that wondrous godly tongue, should ne'er get defiled
with dirt of earth (low laughs, they meant) but sorely glow

with soul's fine inward glance, flow with tears' hot brine,
em-pedestal each sniffle . . . unto by-gosh tragic!
Thus reasoning, they sharpened petty tines
to jab him who'd inserted low comic magic

into ethereal, sidereal poetic lines.
Their tines stayed blunt, wouldn't you know it?
Thence those sad poets sought refuge: *Milton stayed blind*
(and unread by them!) *so let us stow it,*

our disdain, we mean, and regain our sniffles.
How pretty they lie! Sublime pain, how they show it!
. . . So said, their lives continued without a ripple.
His, howe'er, tottered. *Thalia,* he cried, *you know it*

to be unjust and rank that my hymn to you
so sprawled ignored, maligned. Instead of praiseflow,
it received but scorn for its rhyme and vision true.
Her reply? In these dark times dare she let it show?

Sure: *Out your poetic asses, won't all of you blow?*

4

Chapter One: The Choice Revealed

Herein, Shades inhabiting the underworld of Hades upheave over the perfidy on earth above. Hoping to restore a modicum of political peace to their living progeny, they appoint one of their own to return amongst the living. The Greek Diogenes, in eternal lantern search for one honest man, announces that Lord Hades has chosen Victoria Woodhull, the proponent of free love who once ran for President of the United States, to undertake this immense peace-making task. Dio's somewhat faithful Doberman Pluto seconds the motion with a playful howl.

We open in a deep and cranky underworld
to hear Apple earbuds vibrate this fearful sound:
On earth above, such chaos hath unfurled!
Let us arise and aid our progeny, fix them aground!

"*Send Abe!*" some gave shout. "*Send Plato!*" cried others.
"*Churchill!*" wailed many. "*Gandhi!*" some did plead . . .
A lantern glowed. In aged hand, it hovered.
"Diogenes," whispers came, taking seed.

All underworld eyes focused upon that glow,
all underworld hands splayed, open and ready,
all underworld ears pricked, ready to know
the choice of this searcher, infinitely steady.

From a dais, he coughed just twice, his preamble.
"Victoria," he announced, brown Greek eyes a-blink. /
"That stuffy queen?" This dismayed reply gave amble
through red underworld grass whilst doubters sipped their drink,

ambrosia its name, more mickey finn
its fame. "No, no, not her. She's much too much in snit
about Elizabeth's longevity. Shall it not end?"
Diogenes smiled and did his lantern bit.

"Woodhull," he announced. /
                              "Who?" faces below shouted. /
"You've seen her." D did a boy thing with cupped hands
at his chest. Females rolled their eyes. Who had doubted
this new next world would toss but the same? Angel bands?

Ha! Just sex-crazed old men in search of Viagra.
A pharmacist down here could attain a fortune. /
"She's got brains! Gumption enough to stagger a
red state or blue," D added, perceiving the tune

his antic hands had spurred. *En masse*, the females
exhaled: "Two millennia searching for an honest
man—at last, he's willing to try us." /
                              "He wails
about no candid caps. Let him try a bonnet." /

"Have you seen her? She's awfully haughty." /
"She ran for President before Clinton, Thatcher,
Meir were sprouted." /
                     "I heard that she was naughty." /
"Yes, her free love, I heard it too." /
                              "Well, our rapture

gave end to that." The ladies looked askance
toward that last speaker. "Well didn't it?" /
Their silent answer locked them each in trance.
Diogenes spoke wind with words bidding it—

their silence, that is—to stay: "She has her faults.
Of that I'm certain. Let the . . . woman
who hath none shift my choice hard into halt."
He glanced about, playing the showman.

Nor a ruffle, nor a murmur, nor a cough.
"Well then, Victoria Woodhull it is.
Come. Gather. I'll disclose directives from the loft
of ol' Hades himself, our leader, that whiz.

"A-wooo!" D then howled. No sooner howled than done:
a Doberman of tawny hue ran to his side.
"Woof!" Pluto replied. Folk gathered for the fun.
D and his dogs always supplied a raucous ride.

D felt the great crowd below jostle his platform.
Then movement he spotted, distant, off yonder.
Persephone? Way early for her to perform.
Looked like some other crowd mustering. He wondered:

How very oft' such crowds congealed above, then blundered.

Chapter Two: Diogenes Delivers the Summons

Diogenes delivers Lord Hades' appointment to Victoria, who recalls her betrayal by the women's movement, including Elizabeth Cady Stanton, Susan B. Anthony, and Harriet Beecher Stowe—and topping this, her time, courtesy Police Commissioner Comstock, in Manhattan's infamous prison, The Tombs, unjust retaliation for rightfully exposing in her newspaper, Woodhull & Claflin's Weekly, *the famous preacher Henry Ward Beecher, who predated on his female parishioners, privately practicing what she publicly taught: free love. She fears that things will once again go awry in much the same way. Despite her doubts, Diogenes (whom Victoria still mistakenly believes to be Demosthenes) convinces her to accept Lord Hades' summons and return to the land of the living.*

"Demosthenes, is that you?" Though her voice called
uncertainly, a husky timbre combed it.
Diogenes mentally caterwauled:
For over ninety years this woman had roamed it,

the spirit world, that is, but had she as yet learned
his name? No. Some barrier—who to blame but her nasty kin,
in whom concupiscence, calumny, and greed all burned
to sour her grapes, e'en as they gave seed within?

Yet she remained Victoria Woodhull, though oak
and cedar oft' leached from that "hull" to leave soft pine.
A pun. His weakness. "Yes, Vickie, I. Once more folks
above—" /
            "Will anything work right this time?"

The youthful woman literally spat this out.
D spotted a gob near his left sandal.
Well good, she'd attained a fine young body to flout.
From what he'd seen above, she'd need one to handle

up top's political divide. In the USA,
in everywhere, hatred's angst throbbed the air.
All sides hoped to stun opposing bluesters away
with prisons, exile, death—thus lay enemies bare.

Life perched unbalanced, entangling every yoga
guru around. D sighed: They who know not history,
stand doomed to repeat it. One more stained toga,
bloodied. From whence-the-knife-came's the only mystery:

From the Rich and Few, or the Poor and Many?
The right so fire red, the left so blue blue?
CEOs so new, grunt workers so plenty?
Young versus old? Races of every angry hue?

Each side gave flurry like dandelion seeds in wind.
He looked: Vickie's doubt still showed, her question nestling.
But lo! Were not her eyes regaining spark? They could send
a doubter down in life, pinned as if in wrestling.

If only she would take a walkabout to see
sweet rays of hope, like his lantern, still glimmering.
Yes! Faith could move both mountains and breasts to the lee;
D glanced back: Yes! Lord Hades' throne was shimmering!

Lord Hades' hopes—were they not? Yes! This go-around
Victoria'd move and shake, incite some cosmic shift
with her free love stance, stuff hate far underground!
Satyrs and nymphs, how they would lubricate the rift!

Of that, Diogenes kept certain. A new leaf,
such was what Lord Hades had flipped over.
The underworld, no longer holding simply grief,
would spread its newfound joy above in clover.

And yet . . . Diogenes moved his lantern high, searching,
searching. "Vickie, for over two millennia, I
have asked the same. Things go almost right, then . . . lurching,
lurching. Might the human condition be to—" /
                                        "Try, try, try . . .

"Right? Crap on that!" V lit a cigarette;
D wrinkled his nose. This cursing and this smoking
were recent nasty habits she had let
come round. Odd, she had shown no such moping

after that lost Presidential nomination
and those two hard stints in Manhattan's Tombs,
plus the snubs of half the British nation.
Whatever came of that abomination from the womb

who sent her to Manhattan's prison? Comstock. Now he mucked
cat litter for minor gods—such was the rumor.
And what of the Beecher preacher who fucked
female parishioners with his holy tumor?

He stood on dank underworld streets begging
for fried chicken, only to be marked by dogs
and tom kittens. Justice at last! Piss on the legging
of him who'd cavorted, that hypocrite hog.

"O Vickie." Diogenes gave sigh. She stood pale
and lovely. He sneaked one peek at her chest.
Whence this afterlife obsession with breasts? Well,
alive he'd slept by night in jugs. (Puns are best;

he smiled at his own.) /
                    "I mean it, Demosthenes.
I will not rise just to jump futile hoops again." /
"Victoria dearest. Set your heart at ease."
Diogenes gave his lantern a fancy spin.

"Women can now vote." /
                    "Yes, but will they?" /
"And they have the Pill. It provides a Will." /
"Really, Demosthenes. Has rhyme become your way?" /
"It has good feel. Makes matters less real." /

"Well, gag me with a maggot." V paused, tugging curls.
"I suppose there's nothing for it. Back to England?"
D slowly shook his head. /
                    "New York then? The New World?"
D coughed, moving mouth behind lantern and hand.

"Al . . . ugh huh." /
                    "Please, Demosthenes. Orate clearly.
It's what you do." /
                    "Alabama. That's the new where."
V's eyelids fluttered. She staggered, she nearly
fainted. She did. When she awoke, her auburn hair

fluffed a "Keep Alabama Clean" trash can. She stared.

Chapter Three: Some Quick Help, Some Confusion, Some Problems, Some More Confusion

Victoria gets beamed up to Birmingham, Alabama, where she mistakenly lands on a municipal trash can, since the teleport machines in Hades are notoriously cantankerous, much like Lord Hades himself. Alonzo Rankin, a Creole known as Lonz, comes to her aid, but he soon flees on seeing a white policeman approach. This policeman, named Smith, in a moment of bravado aims his pistol at Alonzo, but Victoria flirts and calms Smith, who gets a call that there is a disturbance at the Civic Center, and takes his leave. Victoria sets out to find Alonzo and warn him. He, however, informs her that he too is a policeman, though undercover, and that he will have Patrolman Smith notified of such. Alonzo then offers to escort Victoria to the Civic Center, where she hopes to initiate her peace-making mission. Diogenes and his Doberman Pluto notify Victoria through iPhone that they have also arrived up top on earth.

Three flapping ravens watched as Vicki fell headfirst
into a Birmingham municipal trash can.
"Where in hell'd she come from?" The youngest said first. /
"You guessed right," the eldest spoke. "Hades and his tricks again." /

"Whoa there, ma cher! You be okay?" A young brown hand
reached, which Vicki clasped as it pulled her from harm.
Her eyelids gave flutter. "Please help me stand.
So glad you were here. I'm certain I'm charmed."

What a chewy hunk, she thought. *Miscegenation
is surely accepted pleasure these modern days.*
"Young man," she intoned, "I offer the oblation
of feral gratitude, of a fiery love-blaze

"for your coming to my aid." /
                                        "Say what, how?
Cher, your eyes be working all a-fritter." /
"Your skin, so loving brown. From ninety years to now
they've not viewed such virile charm to make them flitter."

Victoria exercised her eyelids once more.
The young man stepped back and pointed to her purse
that lay atop a can of trash. Lord H for sure
had sent it along, as its colors glowed much worse

than ever she might choose: passion red, virgin white.
Oh well, that Lord always claimed his ways were best.
A man in blue—Bright stars, that eternal blight!—
came round a far corner. As if bidden, with zest

her young handsome brown hero wafted down the street.
The officer approached. "That punk botherin' you, Miss?"
He drew a black pistol and took aim at the fleet
brown young man. V, with the softest hand, took his wrist

and fluttered her eyes, wiggled her hips.
Diana forgive me, she thought, *but desperate times,
et cetera*. "Oh no, sir. He helped, for I'd slipped—
perhaps it's the blue sky, perhaps this hot clime—

against your fine municipal trash can."
V rolled a shoulder. The cop lowered his gun
and took lustful note. "Well seein' as you's a 'Bama fan . . ."
V saw the scarlet A on her purse. Hades having fun,

in some Hawthorneian manner? When she got back
she'd make him pay. She pondered her method . . .
For certain: she'd deliver his forked dong a whack
with her black parasol, a gift that rested

near Ye Grande Hot Dog Stand—another of his jokes.
For everyone who was anyone, ambrosia
was the food du jour—either that or tokes.
The cop's two-way crackled. "Lady, I suppose ya

"should take care to avoid that young nigger.
They's not to be trusted at any age."
He put the two-way to his ear. How figure,
V thought, technology grows with a rage,

small voices now squeak from airwaves on high,
but hate against race still keeps its bad broil.
Nigger? You'd have thought that sad word . . . she sighed. /
"Lady, I gotta go. There's some terrible roil

"down to the Civic Center. Gotta keep the peace
in Birmingham." The cop doffed his cap and trotted.
She turned to where the brown lad went. The least
she could do was warn him before this cop spotted

his face again and aimed that nasty black gun.
She hurried that way, thankful she had on sandals,
not those stiff lace-ups that once hid her toes from fun.
No wonder her free love stance had caused such scandals!

Women covered from neck down and corseted . . .
she felt the flow of ruffles about her shoulder,
her hands swept over yoga pants. *We've forfeited*
restrictive clothing! She felt calmer, bolder. /

The three ravens triangulated the cop, the brown guy,
and the running lady. "Oh-ho, this should be fun,"
two spoke in chorus. "Which one plugs which, how, and why?" /
"Leave it. Over there's a fat dead rat, seasoning in sun."

The youngsters realized the wisdom of the older.
All three began to flap, leaving Vicki to trot.
"She's going for that mocha guy, hopes his crank's a boulder." /
"Maybe the other one'll give them both a shot

"from that black pistol." /
                              "Humans! It's always the same old same.
Focus! That rat's been cooling all night and will taste tasty.
Trust me, worrying over humans is lame.
For aging rat meat, though, you gotta move hasty."

V's trot turned into jog, then run. Her arms,
they waved, her fingers tingled, brushing damp hot air.
Her toes gave shout, "Freedom! No more hiding school marms!"
Life these days surely sent something women could bear.

Ahead, the brown lad exited a coffee shop.
She rushed for him, her brain a-whir, thinking of warning.
Her heart too whirred, thinking of a free love hop.
It would be too sad to prop this lad in mourning,

the first nice face she'd met upon her pop
up here onto . . . she slowed her run. *Heavens! It's hot.*
Another of Lord Hades' jokes? She made stop
to shout. Oh my, he stood tall, a butterscotch shot.

"Young man! I come with warning. Don't ever let
that cop see you again. He tried to shoot you,
I'm sure."
        The young man had not yet caffeine-wet
his lovely purple lips, which spoke, "That true?"

He took a coffee sip. "But black lives matter." /
"Well of course," V answered, "as do those of women!
That's why I've come. To stop all this mad hatter
business, restore good life to its purposeful spin."

She raised her face to the lad, he proffered coffee
right back. She took a sip, was not strong and black
but more a mocha cream, even maybe toffee.
A peace offering to prelude a toss in the sack?

V reeled. Her con artist dad, her crazy mother,
her one drunken sis, hot ready to betray,
her other, Tennie, hot ready for a lover,
her husbands wild, sick—no wonder she swerved this way.

But still she straightened her shoulders, resolute.
It must be done, that sublime toss would have to wait.
"The Civic Center. Please point out that institute." /
"They's an art show over there now from Haiti,"

the tall lad said. "I been meaning to go.
I'ma lead you straight that way." /
                          V's eyes lit at his words.
"Wait! That cop's going there too. His gun won't keep stowed." /
A butterscotch smile and ivory teeth purred

this huge surprise: "I be an undercover cop,
Detective Alonzo Rankin." A golden badge
skipped out from his waistband. V was ready to drop
again. She wobbled and thought, *Mayhap I could cadge*

just one more round in handsome bronzed arms. Oh stop it,
she chided herself. "But why then did that man
aim to shoot you?" /
                  "Smith. New and ready to pop it.
Scared too, since his partner got shot. A teensy phone call can

reset his clock." Extruding from his right pocket
a tablet thin and blue, Lonzo pressed it to talk.
His voice soft, technology pure, V's heart locket
clicked open as they began their strident walk.

"Cher, he been told the error of his way. The Center,
though, be having a bad fait: some short guy in brown
down there be screaming 'bout commies like we enter
a funk' time warp. Nowtime, ever'one get down

"like blood and bones hoodoo him—or her—to.
Jesus for some, 'Bama or Voodoo for others." /
Vickie listened and figured it wouldn't hurt to
read a newspaper. Or two. "You have a brother?"

she asked, then slapped her forehead. Oh, focus!
You need facts. Sis Tennie's doing fine in Hades.
Grant, Lincoln, Diogenes fall for her slow hocus. /
"Just three grand soeurs. That be why I loves the ladies." /

"Is your library near the Civic Center?" She
pressed her lips prim while she recalled the three
sole books in Hades: *The Fine Art of Tea,*
Child's Book of Dinosaurs, and some fiddledy dee

entitled *Pineapple.* When she got back she'd do
a dance, enact a protest or three, make the gods
and Hades set loose spirit cash from their flue.
Just three? No wonder everyone down there gives nods! /

"Is kindly near. But I may have duty call,
may have to let Siri lend you her guiding hand." /
"Siri?" This was a goddess V could not recall.
Something rumbled her purse, made visceral demand.

"V? 'Tis I. Where're you? Me and Pluto are on land."

Chapter Four: One More Thing To Bark At

At first Diogenes does not see Victoria, and thinking that Lord Hades is pulling another notoriously bad joke, tries to tug his penis in protest. When living in Athens, this was his favorite ways to dissent, along with sleeping in wine jugs and cavorting with dogs. He is now prevented from tugging by a zipper, something he's never encountered. He soon finds Victoria, but also spots J. Edgar Hoover, who's been beamed up from Hades too. In Hades, J. Edgar spent his time shadowing Marx, Lenin, and Engels, simultaneously asking any Shade he encountered to buy him a gift for his upcoming birthday or anniversary with the Bureau. And of course while alive he railed against communism and Civil Rights "agitators" as if they were one and the same, simultaneously demanding that employees of the FBI buy him gifts commemorating his various milestones with the Bureau. Plus ça change, plus les memes choses. *Hearing Hoover caterwaul against commies at the Civic Center is entirely too much for Diogenes; he suspects some grand Hadeian joke is indeed in the making; he suspects that Hades' show of care for the tumult topside had been entirely show.* Pshaw, in brief.

Hell's Beam-Me-Up-Scotty Machine was often broke.
If Folk complained, Lord Hades' answer was, "Pshaw."
True, 'twas his answer to all, his sick, unkind joke.
So, not seeing Vicki, Pluto just licked his paw

and gave a short rueful bark. Diogenes, though,
tried tugging his wong, thinking an angry jerk
would prove his point. A zipper stopped that show.
D had never felt one. Up here, evil must lurk

if a fellow could not pull out his joint en pointe
in protest. Thus his thoughts, though they lasted not long.
His duty stayed to find V. Somewhere on this joint
she diddled. He grinned at his pun, knowing well her love song

would be ensnaring some handsome rich stud
to aid her mission. Well, Beauty is Truth,
and Truth can always use a quickening of her blood.
He spotted a blinking, scrolling sign. Such bright youth-

fullness played in this land! He donned his glasses,
a gift from Spinoza, who'd approached quite close
to an honest man. D's lantern spurt green gasses
to toast that dead one. The blinking again arose:

B'ham Civic Center. Pluto then gave growl low
at a squat, bulldog-looking guy in brown

who multi-tasked: "These commies!" Howling so
while scribbling index cards consigning those around,

taking special interest in a tall mocha man
of thirty years of growth. Pluto sung out low whine.
"Good pup. I see her," D said. His initial plan
had been to approach Vickie with a lantern shine,

but seeing her lean close to the handsome mocha
gent, he delayed. Whenever Plato'd leaned that way
toward some sweet boy, philosophy would float a
thousand beds away. Even Pluto's bark could never stay

Dame Philosophy. Same show'd go, he knew, with V.
Wait! The brown-suited bulldog guy looked familiar.
Of course. He sneaked about in Hades, climbing trees,
scratching notes on Marx, Lenin—enough to fill your

greenest Dempsey Dumpster to its brim and more.
Damn it, Lord Hades! This isn't one bit funny!
Why'd you beam this J. Ed creep up to Terra's shore?
Wasn't Vickie's task to turn folks up here sunny?

Diogenes could spot no jug to hole up in,
so he yipped, he pranced, he hopped himself sore.
He barked, he howled. Embarrassed, Pluto rolled up in
a curl, to do his best, his master to ignore.

Meantime, the brown-suit guy was giving a doozy
of a show, shrilling out notes from index cards:
that such a woman was both commie and floozy,
that pinko leanings could be found in Britain's Bard,

that America's N double A C and P
booked cruises to Russia, that SCLC
came not from Atlanta but the Commie Red Sea.
The suited guy stopped, spotting Pluto running free.

He gave a smile, then walking to pet Pluto's head,
announced, "We should all love our dogs. They can't be Red."
He pulled a treat deep from his pants; a card got shed.
Pluto gobbled the treat, ignored what the nutcase said.

The lantern in D's hand swayed as he plucked the card
to read, "The latest poop on the second Judge Bean?
He yaps about Jesus but look in his back yard:
it's fourteen-year-old girls who make him scream."

The brown-suited man spoke, "J. Edgar Hoover is my name;
putting down commies and trash is my game."
J. Ed gave squint at D's lantern. "Friend, don't cause shame:
you aren't no weird intellectual posing that flame,

"are you? I mean, something tocks off about them.
Instead of Red they see pink, instead of black and
white they see whore gray. Unworthy to touch the hem
of Liberty's skirt, they should be stacked to stand

"on a cattle boat bound for Russia. —Hey, today's
my birthday. Buy me a gift. I spotted a smack
Tiffany lamp in a shop not too far away."
Pluto tilted his head, D jerked his lantern back.

Would this fruitcake ruin Victoria's show?
D looked: beady eyes, thinning hair, bulldog chops.
Well, V was a fruitcake too, truth to be told.
D's lantern sputtered. Indeed, all humans were flops

if you studied hard to it. That Darwin fellow—
survival of the mostly fit? No earthly way.
But his mutation part sat just right. Goes to show
how humans can spot one aspect of the Grand Guignol Play.

Mutation, rotation, constipation,
inflation, degradation—all get ovation
from the grand jeté chaos plies on every nation,
thus lofting whims, emotions high unto logic's station.

Was enough—almost—to halt his lifelong search.
More than lifelong, truth be told. He gave a playful
sway to his lamp as a uniformed cop gave lurch.
A sputter, of course—and one somewhat hateful.

"I mean it! I turned one hundred-twenty today!
Folks, isn't that just grand? Commies and malcontents—"
The rookie who'd almost shot Alonzo away
eyed them both with a satchel of blustery intents.

"Say, mister. Dogs all gotta stay on a leash.
And you, bud, we don't 'low panhandling in this town." /
"Officer, everyone knows me. My Bureau's reach
covers this grand breadbasket land, from up to down.

"J. Edgar Hoover's my name. Commies stay my game." /
Smith—yes, 'twas he—scowled. "That guy's been dead fifty years." /
"While communism's alive, I thrive. That's my fame." /
A teen boy gave shout, "All them Reds is dead. No tears

"was shed. My granddad said that, and he fought in Nam."
D and Pluto, during this high discourse, gave search
for a Beam-Me Machine. Their eyes at last did glom
on one disguised as a Port-o-Let. In a lurch

like this, it shone sacred as a snake handler's church.

Chapter Five: Interlude in Hades

Diogenes and Pluto travel back to hell to protest to Lord Hades about the presence of J.
Edgar Hoover, who will surely thwart any peace-making plans Victoria enacts.

Diogenes gave tug quite fierce to his zipper:
no show, no go. On seeing Lord Hades' sly grin,
he rolled these words out: "My wong could be a fish's flipper
for all this contraption's worth! I can't make it spin!

"Your so-called honest messenger, slick Mercury,
gave promise that Dame Vickie was being beamed
to lend her aid. Please do imagine her fury
when she spots that Hoover beast who's never been weaned

"from chasing after boogie bear commies.
For sure she'll pop hard thwacks on your forked dong."
Small joy to D when Hades covered his tommy.
D'd heard it slung as forked as his hung long.

Great Zeus! Focus, he chid himself. *No wonder*
your lantern can't cast its beam on some honest
soul, when its sway-swinger sings with such sore blunder!
D moved his Greek shoulders back. However long it

took, he'd find one honest creature! "Do you hear me?!"
he shouted at Lord Hades, who'd moved to trimming
his talons. "My lantern will shine and will steer me
toward one honest human who's not a lemming." /

Lord Hades flicked a cobby nail at the Greek. /
"Have you no empathy!? No soft feeling!?
Just beam me back up! The humans above all seek
your guiding hand. And what! You toss a nail peeling!?

"Can you not rather send them some hopeful answer?"
Diogenes bent for the jagged coal black claw,
then tugged the zipper hasping his woeful pants sure. /
Lord Hades grinned his fangiest grin, then hissed, "Pshaw."

Just what D expected: the Universe, ruled by flaw.

Chapter Six: Back in the Hot Ham

Diogenes returns to Birmingham, his pleas having been ignored by Lord Hades. Yet Diogenes feels compassion for Victoria and is willing to help her as he can. Besides, he still is searching with his lantern for one honest (hu)man. As Diogenes expected, however, Hoover and Victoria clash, though Victoria does manage to initiate four teenage girls into her free-love stance as modern, though steaming, Furies.

By the watch he didn't wear, the lantern he held,
Diogenes figured four minutes had passed
from taking his trip to Hell. Up top, V was set to melt,
for she'd ID'ed the Hoover creep from hell's deep gas.

She stood stamping her feet, then tugging her sandals,
yanking each off to toss at the commie-chasing fellow.
The tall mocha cop reached out to handle
her pending mistake, e'en as Hoover gave bellow.

"Nice lady, don't ruin your pretty green shoe.
Besides, ol' Smith would have to haul you in
for disturbin' the peace. You don't want in that crew
down the jailhouse. Ain't no pretty sight, loads of sin."

Dame Vickie was too tough to cry, but she could wail.
"I'm here to spread love's peace. What do I get?
Some dog-faced idiot emptying his foul pail
of hate and fear!" /
                              "Those faults lie with the other set!"

J Ed's bulldog chops allowed. "The agitators
who want to pull America fast crumbling down!
We need stout-hearted men, not low imitators!" /
V bristled. "Stout men? And what of women, you clown?" /

"My momma, my two nieces, Miss Helen Gandy—
they were plenty stout. And they knew their place!" /
The mocha man couldn't stop the sandal handy
to V; it wound up smacking J Ed in his face.

Was good that rookie Smith was inspecting
Pluto's leash and rabies tag, just made in Hades,
else he'd follow protocol and be directing
V to jail. He treated gents the same as ladies:

bad was bad was bad was bad, whether it put on
a jock strap or a sandal. Let them cool their clits
and tits, penises and gonads in jail! Rut on
that! Do think upon the Good Sweet Lord for a bit!

What would Jesus do? Punch these perverted deep creeps
in their non-human snouts! Send them to burn in hell!
Satisfied with Pluto's tag and leash, Smith gave peep
to the panhandler who had commies for sale. /

"Look in your attic! Look under your bed!
They're sneaking, they're lurking, cupping Marx in their hand!
I've read him, I've heard him, he's a gosh-darned Red!
They want—believe me!—to put *Pravda* in our land!

"My birthday—did I tell you?—it's today.
Right by that lamp sits an antique G-man poster.
Ah, tommy guns, molls, and mobsters, such good old days!
One year, the guys bought me an autographed holster;

"John Wayne himself inscribed it, 'For a true patriot!'" /
These words gave rookie Smith a pause in snooping.
This loon had John Wayne's autograph? That made a fat lot
of cognitive assonance! A good less drooping

now played about the oldster's jowls. Oh hell, let him howl
about commies, reds, and that whoever guy Marks.
For sure plenty other things were going fowl
and needed tending: that barefoot woman with sparks

in her eyes, for one. What was she stirring up now,
there talking with four teenage girlies? Commotion
elsewhere caught his eye. Four guys straight off the plow
jostled a bum, then bobbed like Atlantic ocean

waves to shout, "Plug Reds in the head! Blast them all dead!"
The four teen girls gave counter, "Make love and hug forever!"
Smith glanced at his watch, felt a sprinkle on his head.
Storm brewing, shift nearly over: time to sever.

A nod to the mocha guy: Smith's goodbye lever.

Chapter Seven: The Lantern Don't Lie

Matters in front of the Civic Center escalate mightily. Victoria's four big-city Furies side against four male farm boys—soon to be enjoined by hundreds of teens arriving early for a rock concert. To escalate matters, a newly arrived troublemaker, Judge Roy Bean Too, arrives on the premise, having been rejected by a fourteen-year-old teen's mother at the Galleria's food court, so now searching for a delectable teenage girl at this concert. Victoria, meanwhile, espies J. Edgar's violet toenail polish and guesses the implications, but in a moment of empathy lets the secret go.

Alonzo was partly right: the Haitian art show
had closed the night before. Now two rock stars
were heading the venue, hence the teeny-bop glow.
By Zeus's beard! The lot was filled with fancy cars!

"Make fug, not war!" /
                    "Let America hate again!"
That, the two foursomes still at it, F versus M.
Each faced off other, spittle flecking their chins.
As more teens gathered, lending the area vim,

J. Ed and Vicki threatened tailspin:
J. Edgar glared at V; V glared back at him.
A screech! V's second sandal clubbed J. Ed's chin.
J. Ed searched for his tommy gun, though hope went slim

when he remembered it lay encased in walnut
in his man-basement on Thirtieth Place Northwest.
It was the one that blasted Dillinger's fall, but
its bullets languished there so long, molding in rest,

they likely could swoosh at best. He spied a spin—
that lantern, swinging in the old geezer's hand!
"Make fug, not war!" /
                    "Let America hate again!"
With it, he could smash the wench's overwrought glands.

"Make fug, not war!" /
                    "Let America hate again!"
Sublime the music those yelps did make. No protest,
he figured, but glad parade. No commie sin,
but patriotic youth, glowing their U.S. best.

"Make fug, not war!" /
                    "Let America hate again!"
Quite soon that rhythm also made Vicki sway.
Alonzo and Smith couldn't resist; they joined in.
Passers stopped, such charm within the melody lay.

"Make fug, not war!" /
                    "Let America hate again!"
Democracy and Twitter were having their say.
"Make fug, not war!" /
                    "Let America hate again!"
75, a 100 joined as if to flay

common sense, logic, empathy, and other words
esteemed—so claimed!—by the species called sapient.
Truth is, those thoughtful modes evoke but bile and gerds.
'Tis passion sets our teeth to gnash, brows to furl, eyes to glint.

"Make fug, not war!" /
                    "Let America hate again!"
Inside, the bands were practicing; outside, sound waves
made fugue as if Bach himself had zeroed them in.
A *Rolling Stone* music critic would expound raves.

Diogenes swung his lantern wildly about.
Amidst these youngsters, might just one not tainted,
with honest song sing out? Might this day send something but rout?
Left, right, right, left, he swung, he swung. Then he fainted.

"Make fug, not war!" /
                    "Let America hate again!"
Clomp! Clomp! Was odd, but boots composed the footwear du jour
for most teens here. J Ed gave V's sandal a spin,
removed his fine brown wing-tips with hands manly sure,

and be-clonked V twice on her own dimpled chin.
Feeling victory, J Ed tugged off his argyles.
Ten violet toenails glowed; Vicki gave a grin.
"Mistake! My two young nieces!" J Ed faked wee smiles.

"Make fug, not war!" /
                    "Let America hate again!"
Vicki inspected the wing-tips, proffered them back.

"Make fug, not war!" /
        "Let America hate again!"
The poor thwarted fella, she'd cut him some slack.

Elsewhere, food fights turned passé. Change just two letters . . .
Voila! Boot fights. Amid that stink, which side could win?
Boots got tossed, feet got kicked, socks turned to fetters.
Two hundred joined now in fray; love took bi-pedal tailspin.

Toenails jabbed and sliced, toe jam oozed distressing;
Athlete's foot slew many, others got felled by crabs or lice.
For preschoolers it would have been impressing;
for supposed adults, it just didn't seem nice.

Callused heels kicked out hard, pink corns gave whinny.
Some feet shown cotton white, some tanning spa tan;
some blisters popped—but these were teens, so not many;
some glowed African black, some many colors spanned.

One college teen had moved down from ol' Kentucky,
where walking barefoot in bluegrass had lent her worms.
Whomever she kicked at stayed quite lucky,
for her every thrust was telegraphed by squirms.

A lad from Tuscaloosa'd come to see the band.
Removing his Nikes—where were his boots?—
he spied a Dear John note amid Gulf Shores sand.
Your drinking, Frankie, flings ungodly. You have no roots.

A tear crept behind his eye; he tugged at a pint
of Maker's Mark and flung his tennie at a senior
from Hoover High. She caught it, straightened her spine,
then grabbed his booze to shout, "Go find the Lord! Wean yer-

"self off this Devil's brew." /
        "Jesus freak!" he shouted.
"Better Jesus than dialysis!" /
        "Huh?" said he.
"Big word for a college guy?" /
        Frankie sat routed;
still he hurled his second Nike with wholesome glee.

Sweet Liza, come up from Sumter County,
tugged off her dancing boots with silver frills.
She hurled them at two twins—bonus bounty!
They dodged and gave sweet Liza two fingers with trills.

Savaté—French Kick Boxing—came close enough
to Euro flair for this mad scene. Some gagged from smell;
some whimpered just from shouts (their home life being rough);
chaos took some, who tripped over a boot and fell.

"Make fug, not war!" /
                    "Let America hate again!"
The eternal gong gonged them on. Biff, Kick, and Boom!
Each head mushroomed in hatred's frenzied spin.
Judge this unfit for great outdoors? Best spun in dark, dank rooms?

Just think: Shiloh with spring, Normandy with summer,
Hiroshima with morn, Nagasaki with lunch;
Stalingrad with snow—dear Zeus, they're all a bummer!
Indoors or out, mankind's a teeny-bopping bunch.

Diogenes stirred; he stood tall, where air flowed fresh.
Something approached; his lantern's flame whistled.
Was this immortal, or simply a man of flesh?
Its beady eyes made Diogenes bristle . . .

still, the lantern must be allowed to reveal
each soul's truthful state: will it show high, or lowly sink?
D lurched to save his lantern from a tossed boot heel,
which flew on by. He raised the lantern above the stink . . .

Lo! It revealed cowboy boots slick-oiled and shiny.
The light reflecting off them—Zeus's will be done!—
seemed mountain river pure, not Gulf Coast briny.
Just what did here approach? A demi-god battling in sun?

A gentleman's gentleman, suave in Southern ways?
A peacekeeper, a heart's ease and learned guru?
A lawgiver, remindful of Solon's days?
A legal leader, uplifting code so we might see true?

Behold! Judge Roy Bean Too, arrived fresh from court—
food court in the Galleria, just to make clear—
where a young teen's momma had made him abort
his social plans for her fourteen-year-old dear.

"That old guy Joe and that young virgin Mary
got it on," he'd argued. "Check your family Bible."
When Mom pulled out her mace, the judge did not tarry,
but drove Civic Center-ward, where he felt liable

to snare a lonesome teen. Should he pack his gun?
Jesus snapped whips and threw rocks at the whore,
so sure.
                    Once there, the judge sniffed the foot-fighting fun.
My Lord! Someone should franchise a Desenex store.

When he tugged his boot to join in, a lantern swung
right by his face. "By high god Zeus," its swinger said,
"a wonder the glass didn't break." A boot got flung
betwixt them both. It smelled of something longtime dead.

Truth told, the whole area now smelled of carrion.
It's said that three things lubricate good friends:
five-course meals, amour, and whiskey. Nary a one
of those did hover o'er the plaza to bend,

But wait! Rita's Hot Dog Van pulled in. Could weenies allay?
Teens grabbed their boots and rushed her way. Not a one
would squinch a nose effete at onions or chili that day.
Even sauerkraut spread vibes of peace under the sun.

Logic, zip. Passion, zip. Hunger and stink doth overcome.

Chapter Eight: The Pro Anti-league Colludes

After the melee in front of the Civic Center, Judge Roy Bean Too and J. Edgar Hoover confabulate in a secluded spot, where the two of them blithely ignore one another's perceived flaws to further their egos and their ambitions.

The judge's jowls had found camaraderie with those
of J Ed. They wobbled, each to each, they gathered
in a concrete niche, thrust as deep as violet toes.
Within those shadows both felt comfy. They'd lathered

politico collusion plenteous enough. They too
knew hawks from handsaws, or even sparrows.
"My name's J Edgar Hoover. I'll shut down any screw
commie, gangster, druggie with smelly marrow,

Lindbergh kidnapper, civil rights agitator,
perverted child molester."
⠀⠀⠀⠀⠀⠀⠀⠀⠀⠀⠀⠀⠀⠀⠀⠀With that last phrase,
the good judge's eyes whirred as if some dilator
got dropped in them. Recovering, he seemed unfazed.

"Name's Judge Roy Bean Too. I hate unbelievers, liberals,
college professor trash, them same agitators,
bad gamblers, drinkers, a homasex'al who mulls
to make itself a holy marriage imitator—

all them faggots and more."
⠀⠀⠀⠀⠀⠀⠀⠀⠀⠀⠀⠀⠀⠀⠀⠀With that last phrase,
J Edgar's eyes whirred as if some dilator
got dropped in them. Recovering, he seemed unfazed.
"My friend," he told the judge, "we should send those traitors

"to terminal jail." /
⠀⠀⠀⠀⠀⠀⠀⠀⠀⠀⠀⠀"Jail's too good. Crucify them!" /
"The Constitution that may not allow." /
⠀⠀⠀⠀⠀⠀⠀⠀⠀⠀⠀⠀⠀⠀⠀⠀⠀⠀"A judge
can always rewrite evil laws, loosify them,
then chip some better into granite that won't budge,

"just like those Commandments Ten high up on the Mount." /
"America could use a Prez like you.
Let's put our queer shoulders to the wheel and give it bounce."
J Ed, no Greek, *could* blush. He did. The judge changed hue.

Though J Ed's gaff came abrupt, narcissists stay true.
They both smiled teeth, and hands they shook, fine Southern gents
who'd never peep in mommy's closet where great slews
of secrets hid amongst skirts, jars, and brooms. Both kept intent

on their anti-goal goals, both vowed to not relent.
"You stand a man I trust!" they ballyhooed.
Their deal was struck; it glowed, Hades-sent.
Two cigars were lit, the smoke of which arose to rue

three ravens and two teens prone on ledges overhead.
The ravens were digesting the deceased rat;
the teens twisted and squirmed to prove they weren't dead.
Each group ignored the other: 'twas one of life's facts.

But both above did pause to hear what below got said.
The teens held deep breaths galore from osculation;
the ravens cawed koans about life from the dead.
When cigar smoke rose to climax below's conversation,

teens kissed; ravens gracked; the adults just sent aggravation.

Chapter Nine: One Lantern-light Consult, One Miss

Victoria tells Diogenes about J. Edgar's probable homosexual leanings, and in good nine-teenth century fashion blames such on J. Edgar's mother. She gets quickly reprimanded for this conjecture by Dr. Eddie Truelove, head of UAB's renowned neuroscience depart-ment. Soon enough, Doc Eddie, having been raised on Sand Mountain, identifies both Diogenes and Victoria as "haints" returned from death. Additionally, he identifies Dio-genes by his lantern. Victoria is mortified that she has mistaken Diogenes for Demosthenes for well over a century. Alonzo comes upon the group and recognizes Doc Eddie from his forensic work with the Birmingham police. Victoria and Diogenes cover with white lies when Doc Eddie starts to reveal their true identities.

The lady's hot dog stand made D check his middle:
encasèd still. He shined his lantern there to find
blockades most cruel of intricate, linkèd metal.
Protesting bad justice by giving his wong wind

seemed hardly possible. And while *he* had no need
of watery elimination—ambrosia saw to that—
what of the living crew up here? Just how they peed
imposed unthinkable mystery. Might ever he solve that?

He spied Victoria tapping grit from her sandal.
She smiled. "Did you see my red-headed Furies?
Those four will lend justice a wholesome handle." /
Harpies, more like it, D thought. For sure he

kept his mouth as mute as his dong. "Hard to miss them,"
was all he offered. "But what happened to your gent?" /
"I cannot tell. A gal could get bliss from him,
though he's a cop, you know, hardly my usual bent." /

"Never should you, V, judge a book by its cover." /
"Indeed . . . you want to give him the ol' honest lantern test?"
V sent a grin. "I'd be pleased to let him hover
o'er me while you did. I'd even lie prone in rest."

With titters, Vickie sucked the last of her hot dog.
Lasciviously. Then she proffered a pop
and slurp, wet and loud enough to send hot flog
to guys who stood by, give the gals a gleeful hop.

Diogenes closed his eyes, raised up the lantern
to his forehead. /
                    "Don't pull that virgin act with me!
I've seen you ogle Tennie. Each male shade in turn
roasts and burns for her—except maybe J Ed. He

"wears violet toenail polish, did you see? Poor lamb.
His ma must have hoodooed some fancy frippery
for that to come about. I mean—" /
                              "Excuse me, ma'am,
for listening, but your thought process runs slippery.

"Homosexuality slides up from the genes,
for the most part, that is." /
                    Diogenes spun
his lantern toward the speaking dark-haired man; D's spleen
did spring in hope eternal. Could this be The One?

He held back to examine the loose-framed guy:
black hair curling, a sprinkle of gray for wisdom,
his corner lips turned high—though not so blessed high
to indicate insanity, but to lend some

ironic notion from his teeming mind. D edged
the lantern forth. The man stepped nimbly out of range.
"Dr. Eddie Truelove is my name. I've wedged
neurons and axons enough in my days that strange

"keeps never foreign. Still, something's a-glow with both of you.
My momma hailed from Sand Mountain, where haints abound.
Snake handlers too. Take up serpents, turn yourself blue.
Got bit by a rattler when I was a teen, down—"

the doctor pointed to his thigh. "But ma'am, alack,
that bite nor Momma turned me gay. Genes keep their sway."
V looked up. D stepped forward. Doc stepped back.
"Did not think I'd find haints on my midday sashay,"

the happy doctor said, his eyes going narrow. /
"We . . ." /
          "We . . ." /
                    "No need to deny. I've got Momma's blood,
that snake's, too. I know a handsaw from a sparrow.
Shakespeare, I think. He still play below in your hood?"

"We . . ." /

      "We . . ." /

             "Either haints or loonies. Care to visit
my lab, undergo an FMRI?
Imagine what papers I'd write, all from kismet—
Say, I bet you're Diogenes. Your lantern's why

"that thought came—But you, ma'am, so ill-informed yet fair?" /
Vickie blinked at the lantern. "Diogenes? Can
that be right? Not Demosthenes whom my life shared,
who spirit-led me through arrests, protests, my clan?" /

Greeks don't blush, or D would have. "Vickie, I've been
forever trying to tell you that fact." /
"Vickie?' the doctor inserted. "The wrestler I've seen
my momma watch on TV? But muscles you lack,

"so I think not. And that V's still out there living."
This doc, he had a twitch that strolled along one eye
to dance quite hard when heavy thought he got giving. /
"Diogenes?" V persisted. "That weird Greek guy

"who'd yank his peter in public, who slept in jugs?
Why didn't you say so in the first place? You'd fit
right in with my kin." /
             Doc Eddie's eye twitched his mug.
This underworld mis-communication had lit

a bonfire in his mind. "Why sure! This all syncs in.
Emotions yank us about up here while we're alive,
so emos would still yank haints below, put kinks in
famed logic.—Please! Let me try an FMRI!"

Doc Eddie's clothing hung so limp and loose
that one need search to find his stethoscope and tie.
His facial hair slung thin and mossy, like a moose.
His skin, it flaked pale, dry. But his thoughts flung so high,

and he moved so bouncy with excitement that D
was able to shift his lantern near . . . It sputtered.
D's Greek shoulders fell: at least one outward sign he
did share. Calm Pluto rubbed D's leg whilst he muttered

in disappointment. 'Twas something miraculous,
D's never-say-die hope, 'twas like gun-control folk,
or Cubbie fans, or teachers—almost crapulous
from obsession, yet their burdensome yolk

tugs them as hard as they tug it—toward nowhere.
"Awooo!" Diogenes howled. "Awooo!" echoed
Pluto, the Doc, and V. Sad stayed somewhere all four could share.
Their chorus attracted Alonzo, who soon showed

to ease their grief with goodwill and coffee plenty.
He toted four in a tray, one extra lest he
despoil some unannouncèd guest, this a bent he
shared with Romans and their "Unknown God." At best he

gave swill to strangers, at worst he drank more caffeine,
nothing odd for a cop. "Say, I know you!
You be the doc brought in when bad guys' brains churn lean." /
"What about bad gals?" V asked sipping from the brew. /

"Oh sure, some of them too." Alonzo smiled. "But you,
dear cher so charm', could never bounce with that sad group." /
V blushed, was something she practiced and could do
with ease. /
           Doc Eddie said, "To get you in the loop,

"this gent here is—" /
                  "Dio the Greek. My sweet pop fishes down
in Tarpon Springs. I'm here to visit my fine young friend."
Diogenes turned to V, who turned *him* a frown. /
"And *you're* on search for one honest man? White lies send

impure vibrations—truth is, kind sir, he's godfather
to me. He tries his best to keep me from the arms
of handsomes like you. He really shouldn't bother."
Flirt begets flirt, V thought. *Little lies, little charms.* /

"And your name, wondrous one?" Alonzo proffered back. /
"Vickie Bush," she replied with a giggle.
"No kin to George or W. Nope, presidents lack
in my family tree."
                At this, D's lantern wriggled.

Its movement sent him forth to check out the mocha
guy, who proved alert enough to skip back, though still
balancing his last coffee on his tray. No one spoke a
word. Each brightly drank caffeine enough to drill

each lie they'd heard. Beware! Like coffee hot, such lies might spill.

Chapter Ten: To the Library

Dropped off at the Birmingham Public Library by Alonzo, Victoria and Diogenes gain entrance despite Pluto and the lit lantern. Once again, a melee quickly develops as Fake News gets propagated about Disney and Donald Trump, proving that the Underworld rumors about chaos rising amongst the living stand too very true.

Before Doc Eddie renewed his midday ramble,
he made certain to leave his contact with all three.
Alonzo, who had parked in nearby street bramble,
said he'd drive V and D where they might read and see

what current events flipped my country 'tis of thee.
"So handsome," Dio backseat-whispered to Vickie. /
"Mmm," came her sibilant reply. Great Zeus, but she
and her mid-bod pulsed all warm and slippery

as she leaned on into Alonzo's comfy ride. /
"Next week back there, a musical, *The Lion King.*
S'posed to be 'bout Africa. Why?" Alonzo sighed.
"The weather here hot enough to make chickens sing.

"As hot as that lantern you carry, pops."
Lonz glanced back. "Dites-moi, what you do with that thing
anywoo?" /
                "It's a love meter, saves hearts from flops,"
Vickie offered. "Which means it takes away the sting

"of sweet amour not flowing right." /
                                    "I coulda used
that 'bout ninety-'leven times, strap it on my shoe." /
"*Truth* is what it measures," yelped D. "Which gets abused."
He snapped this out, angered by Lonz and V's flirty stew.

Still, he thought, *you never know,* so he leaned
the lantern. Just then they took a curve;
the lantern swayed into Pluto, whose honest sheen
sent it aglow. But only humans could serve

to make the honest test true. /
                              "Truth," V asserted,
"it's such an odd concept. Kind sir, you stand—or sit—"
she giggled, "an example fine. Unless you'd alerted
me, I'd never known exactly how your candle lit."

Diogenes scowled at Vickie's poor pun. His eyes gave flit. /
"Ah la, always poor truth be to take some beating,"
Alonzo inserted. "Tout ça fake news put me in snit." /
A backseat bump from Pluto nudged the lantern, though fleeting

time and brakes sent Alonzo forth. "Library ahead.
I stop and let toutes vous off. Like to see you more,
you know? I mean, after you read what you've read." /
Pluto whined, D frowned, V replied, "For sure.

Meeting gives pleasure." /
                                        "Beyond measure," griped D. /
"Shift done soon. I make to drive on back, give you ride." /
A *ride* or **ride**, thought D. *Adult love never comes free.*
Me? I'll sleep alone in some fine wine jug. I keep my pride. /

"Be stopping here." By a hydrant Lonz parked his car.
V got out, sighed, and leaned for a nice cocoa kiss.
Dio pushed his lantern near. Lonz, too fast by far,
made Vickie lurch and the lantern miss,

for Lonzo'd shoved in gear. Still, V did sneak her kiss—
love with light's speed doth always move for certain.
Pluto nudged D, empathic to the lantern's miss.
"Vickie! It might be he! Just keep up your flirtin';

"my lantern will confirm him yet.' /
                                        Dazed, V stood pondering
love and light. Did they move alike? She watched the white
car—a knight up here would not be maundering
any other hue. She checked her purse. *Though crimson is bright*

enough, I guess. She shot a grin. /
                                        "V, work lies ahead.
Turn yourself about. Mankind should be your business." /
"Males I like better. Scrooge and Dickens are dead." /
"As doornails," D responded. "But V, is this

"not what we were sent to do? Mend fences, build trust?"
The library's entrance imposed five feet away.
Magic electric doors slid, sending all three bust:
Pluto barked, V turned pale, D's lantern swayed.

Had Lord Hades sent up trickster door-opening shades?
"Don't worry none," a homeless woman urged. "Catches

me off guard too, each time booze makes its raids
on my matter gray. You might say its slide fetches

my axles and neurals away" (This gal Lena had seen
Doc Eddie for a paid monthly brain-scan study,
she'd picked his lingo up, she even made to preen
it on the street, though mostly she could only muddy

its words and meaning.
                 Of sudden a librarian
gave rush. "Nay, nay! No dogs allowed! Verboten!" /
Homeless Lena proved herself a libertarian:
behind her back she kept a sign she'd been totin':

SURVICE ANIMAL!

She proffered this sign to D. "It's yours for two bills.
With both I'll feed the stray and deserving kitties
who never did nothin' to us. It's our bad wills
keeps 'em yowling and starving. Such a mean pity."

D tugged his wallet. Like V's purse it glowed a crimson *A*.
A passel of bills gushed. As Lena snatched her fill,
D's lantern sputter-judged: No honest gal today.
She ended, "They all deserve the hot dog pill."

D scrunched at Lena's murked said, but fixed the sign on Pluto.
No one emitted howls at this last lantern sputter,
though V did shake her head. Spreading love up here went slow-go.
Bad news was what swept steady. Not an utter

waste though, she recalled with glee: her redhead Furies four
now roamed the land, to spread their love and legs
everywhere, for Everyman. /
                 "Your spelling's poor,"
the librarian hissed. "And that lantern's a keg

"of flame awaiting books. No. Nix. Nein. Verboten!" /
Diogenes lifted his lantern to her face.
It sputtered for sure. /
                 "Oh wait. Forget I've spoken.
Do come in! Books, computers, learning fill this space." /

Vickie and D exchanged glances. Had Lord Hades slipped?
Had he filled the lantern with some peace-making herb,
like a thurible? More probable, this lady'd flipped.
Unlike Hades to change his nasty ways, disturb

the patterns he'd so carefully laid. /
                                        "Oh, do come in,"
the woman gushed again. "What a sweet doggie!" /
Pluto sniffed, uncertain. His hide rippled some in
the oddest place, his right dewclaw. He felt groggy—

mayhap all these books. Could he find tanned leather covers
to tote away to some nice dim corner and chew? /
"Over here are computers, where folks find lovers.
Upstairs we have scads more books, more than a few,

"from subjects arcane to new—I adore your green shoes!" /
V nearly toppled at this. "Best to not look gift
horses in the mouth, unless they come from Greeks, whose—"
she dead-stopped her whisper, fearing a rift

twixt herself and Demos—Diogenes the Greek.
Unknown to them, Library Lady'd spied D's wad of bills.
A donor? Money clanged her mood from rough to meek.
Meanwhile, D schlepped his lantern to a windowsill,

where a bearded gent reeking of wisdom gave nod.
Of course, of course, of course, the lantern sputtered. /
Meanwhile V asked, "Whence newspapers, that current events rod?" /
The librarian tsked. "Just by-gone paper flutters . . .

"what you need, my dear, are Google and Facebook.
Toss in some Twitter and you'll be all set. Let me
show you." She led Vickie to a pleasant nook.
But Lo! There a screen glowed hot, revealing alarming screed!

The librarian stepped back, her shoulders scrunched.
Then forward she leaned, while donning pearled bifocals.
Could what she read be right? All this, well before lunch?
The bright script looked true enough, grammared by yokels:

It linked Prez Trump to a Disneyland Coup.
She tilted her glasses; the screen still blazed. "No! Never!"
she yelled. "My mom and dad live there. This can't be true!" /
"Why, Alice, what's—What!? First they pull the wrong lever,

"and now this? All those fun rides for our sweet children—" /
"That place is full of queers. Oughta be shut down." /
"They won't let guns in there. Carrying's my right, pilgrim! /
"Madmen like you should take your guns and drown!"

The latter clamored by a pale young woman,
the former screamed by a tanned young man.
The two faced off. What might happen, no human gland
could tell. Their libretto posed in unsung plan.

Victoria watched, appalled, her heart giving race.
A lovely teen walked in, her eyes a-glow:
"But *this* is not a mall." She placed hands to face. /
V edged, protective, toward her, amidst the growing row.

This teen though, no help did *she* need. She flipped her skirt
to reveal bright pink panties. One oldster nearby
began to wheeze. He tugged his dank blue shirt.
"Quiet, I'm reading!" He tugged, he squirmed, he gave a sigh.

The screen in question showed Disney's Mickey
yanking Trump's orangutan comb-over,
to flip it on a table, where it ran a tricky
flamboyant circle. The screen then flared: *Disney Takeover!*

A quite literate crowd had gathered, bifocals a-thrum.
They wheezed, they wavered, their fingers gave flutters;
they sniffled, they shouted, their unison undone.
The oldster yelped, "Quiet! I'm reading!" This started mutters.

"That place lets in homos! It even holds a Queer Day!" /
"Caribbean Pirates, that's the best ride there!" /
"Think Trump'll ban it?" /
                    "Ban it, hell! Piracy's his way!" /
"No whiskey, no beer. And you have to share

each line with screaming kids!" /
                    "Quiet! I'm reading!" /
Someone tossed a fat blue dictionary,
which hit the oldster amidst his pleading.
He jumped, he screamed, no more commentary.

He rolled a *Playboy*, searching to deliver a spanking.
A nearby woman inhaled deeply, expelling "For shame!"
Two street bums belched; they then began yanking
books from every which shelf. Though they had poor aim,

more books began to spiral and flip off high shelves,
to drop with bangs. Spines got broken. Pages got ripped.
Alexandria's lost library had never beheld
such horror, though fires and Romans through it had slipped.

One nearby white-haired patron took to time-travel
and ripped her small green bra away. "Give peas a chance!" she yelled.
The teen, who'd come in by mistake, made to unravel
newspapers and magazines; then she too railed,

"Old farts should die, not steal social security!"
One man, searching online for jobs, scraped his chair
to shout that CEOs festered impurity
throughout our land. A dozen then screamed, "Unfair!"

From upstairs, patrons lugged heavy tomes to throw.
From outside, smokers with likewise heavy breath wheezed in.
From bathrooms, break rooms, seekers emitted so's to know
just what would happen when. Each and all, to the fray eased in.

There was no food to throw, and most did not wear boots;
still, soon removed were Crocs, Nikes, sandals, and shoes
to hurl hither, yon. Chairs broke, hair got yanked by roots;
One librarian gave shout, "It's only fake news!"

This increased the frenzy. "Against the President?!" /
"No, posted by that same scoundrel on Twitter!"
The latter from a fella who daily stayed resident
before computers whose frayed wires gave flitter

and sparked at night when the security guard
tapped them to find hot local babes or donate to
the NRA. Lately, life for him had flipped hard:
his girl had turned lesbo, which made him locate to

a straight-guy hovel. Oddly, both these he's
bemoaned the selfsame sit. Odder yet, both their gals
had left them, each for each, judging soft arms would please
far better than gnarly muscles and puerile pals.

A hard-thrown Nike shoe stalled the furor.
It smashed the screen to drop Mickey and Trump
into a powder uniform upon the floor.
V assessed: Was this the final solution? To clump

all aspects of truth into one appeasing, pleasing
scrim? Could her free love message align that task?
Or would it leave matters even worse, heaving
males and females into a roiling flask—not to bask,

but to break and rumble? She thought of her Furies
and smiled. If only those four came cavorting here,
this ragged fight would stop and turn to purely
create a love fest slick and hot enough to sear

hatred's ice into love's warms. Yes! A second paradise!
Free love could parade, it could enchant and sing.
All the world could float, not sink in gravity's vice.
On tippy-toes, V danced and sent her arms to fling.

Then a shoe clomped her ear . . . her head began to ring.

Chapter Eleven: Victoria's Vision

Wherein Victoria, thumped by a heavy shoe, momentarily undergoes a frightening vision.

"Demosthenes, is that you? Are you truly back?
I've had the strangest dream about my dad:
He'd taken Tennie and me, tossed us in a sack.
He bumped us up a stair; he seemed to be glad

as wooden steps clomped our heads and our backs.
He opened the sack in a room of pure scarlet;
he taunted as we cried. Three men sat playing jacks.
Like little boys, they looked up and yelped, 'The harlots

arrive!' They rubbed their penises; then that terrible man
Tom Nast, the one who cartooned me as the wife of Satan,
in through a window gave climb. He cleared his foul, mean glands:
'Strip them, brand them, toss them in our playpen

'with the other mad wenches.' He gave a long twist
to his left moustache, to lend it a phallic curl.
My dad gave thrust to his middle and blew a kiss
at Tennie and me. A scarlet curtain unfurled

revealing a wooden pen designed for swine or cattle,
but painted with barber-pole stripes, in pink and white.
A dozen, ten, bare-breasted women held baby rattles
as men outside gave hue and cry, 'You serve delight!'

These men gave yank to fiery pink members
and spewed hot pale jism inside the pen.
The Beecher preacher and Comstock romped those foul embers.
'You hypocrites!' Tennie and I did vent.

They jigged, they laughed, they ran. 'Delilahs in smock!'
they shouted. Was then I saw Zula my daughter,
her shoulders slumped, standing in tattered shock.
Transported in time, my Furies too awaited slaughter

outside that cattle pen. 'Enough!' I cried.
'Well what?' Comstock replied. 'This is your free love stance.'
'Indeed,' cried Nast, twisting now the right side
of his foul moustache. 'Careless love can only enhance

the fall of women.' /
                    'Of women? Nay of all!'
Comstock insisted. 'Saul—I mean Paul—preaches
that sex is the cause of our first and final fall.
Women should cover nipples and ankles lest leeches

latch on. Procreation is the only pure juice
that should pass betwixt a woman and a man.'
The Beecher preacher flipped up a Fury's loose
red skirt to reveal a hot red thong. 'All Eves must span!'

He threw her hard against the wooden pen;
Comstock grabbed at my daughter Zula for the same.
I grabbed a club, Tennie another, 'Yours is the sin!'
we cried, beating, beating those two men. 'Yours is the shame!'

I woke. Was the club in my hand a penis enflamed?"

Chapter Twelve: The Vision Momentarily Forsaken

Vickie awakens from her vision to espy Alonzo. She voices joy and regret.

Victoria snapped from her dream. What was it all about?
She held a strangely heavy shoe in her left hand.
The phrase "Make hugs, not war!" started out,
but her mouth would not obey that command.

She felt a bump throbbing at her forehead.
She envisioned her daughter and her Furies
imprisoned in that pen. She remembered what Comstock said:
"Sex is the cause of our fall." Would angelic juries

find that the case? The act of love . . . well, wasn't it love?
But yet did sex not slide, did it not slip?
Instead of rising, might it plunge into mud?
Instead of a carrot, might it proffer a whip?

She looked about: that teen girl still rousted, waving her arms.
The oldster with the porn magazine still slumped withering
beneath her stare and that of a silver-haired marm.
But I, Vickie thought, *just sit here dithering.*

She dropped the shoe with a clonk and picked up a book.
To educate well, she knew, one first must learn.
Harry Potter . . . 'twas a children's book from its looks,
Her furies, still children after all: their younger burn

mustn't be pushed onward too fast. The result
would be chaos, like the flood surrounding her now.
She looked about. She spotted her Creole hulk
up front. Forget dreams, there lay the cradle for her bough.

Could she meld pleasure with wisdom? A hard row to plow.

Chapter Thirteen: The Fire Department and Alonzo Arrive

The shoe riot at the library gets dissipated when the fire department arrives. With his lantern, Diogenes tests all the hustling firemen for honesty, with predictable negative results, while musing over Stephen Hawking and Thomas Hobbes. Victoria recruits another Fury by the name of Abby, whom she sends to join her four redheaded Furies. Diogenes at last sneaks his lantern near enough to Alonzo for a test, but discovers its fuel has run out. While a disappointed Diogenes heads back to Hades for refueling, Vickie and Alonzo go search for Judge Roy Bean Too and J. Edgar.

No one had called 9-1-1, despite all the smarm
endured from casting harsh asparagus, one at other.
A tense bag gal, though, had fallen on a fire alarm
to send it ringing. Red trucks arrived to hover,

their hoses a-sprinkle. Ambulances blared.
Even a cop car or two uncovered, which cowed
combatants in there. A glaring, ill-fit peace fared,
steady, but rough.   "If I hadn't already vowed

"to help you spread love, and to find just one honest fellow,
Pluto and I would beam right back." Dio's words made sound
like whimpers in a well, so he hoist a bellow:
"Yo, Vickie! Ol' Plato caused toil enough to stay around

"with his lithe Athenian lads. Can't you leave the boys
alone for thirty secs?" For of course, she'd just spied
Alonzo, and he'd just spied her. To fight their gooey poise,
Dio and Pluto expended not one half a try.

Instead they assessed folk chasing along shelf rows,
the patrons tossing magazines and books,
the firemen in their luminescent clothes—
yes, the lantern was getting a great many looks.

Now and then, down below, the grisly Lord's favorite trick
was quaking Hades till its inhabitants fell seasick
as they rocked to and fro upon the River Styx.
On spotting Alonzo, V had felt her stomach go thick

as if she tossed again on just such a ride.
Oh my, she thought; Alonzo thought, *Such piercing eyes.*
The two bumped hips as booted firemen eased them outside. /
"Hey pops!" one fireman yelled, "you cooking French fries?"

He squirted D's lantern, which, alack, sputtered back:
one more fireman in shiny boots had failed its test.
But Dio gave no time to sighs: more firemen did not lack.
His lantern he thrust, its flame they soaked with zest.

Sputter here, sputter there, his lantern's sputters took no rest;
yet on he thrust, keeping true grit cowboy mode.
Lonesome, hard-nosed, he and Pluto rode erect.
Lonzo's face haunted both: Could one honest man it bode?

Such would be the singularity, not what Hawking preached.
An honest human? Shoot off fireworks! Roast marshmallows!
Parades, please! . . . *But maybe Hawking is right. Computers leech
no human motives hidden, as prescribed that Hobbes fellow.*

Computers glow sure; computers glow pure.
No broken axons, no frayed neuron sheaves.
Solid state, steady state! Logic instant, logic sure!
A wonder to behold, a wonder to believe . . .

But yet, but yet . . . Diogenes and Pluto gave howl.
*Get ready! Get set! Just one is all we need! Billions
and billions, as Carl Sagan says. Don't throw in the towel
with just two short millennia! Not even a million!*

The floor smelled of ozone from busted screens.
Staff and patrons scurried; two mice enjoined their fray.
And yet it's claimed libraries fill our lifelong dreams!
Nope not! If books could trot, they'd have fled too, no delay.

Outside, Vickie bummed a smoke, which sent Lonz to hack.
Dame Vickie gave wink to that selfsame teenage
gal fooled by spacious windows and lured inside, off track—
A new mall's arrived? No, just old folks about! She'd raged:

No Starbucks? Just old farts stealing Social Security?
Now, with impromptu feminist bravado,
she and V huffed streams of nicotine's impurity
at Lonz, who pled, "Cher femmes, this ain't Colorado;

"fresh air be on la premium in the Ham;
steel mill slag and goop still smother about;
up on that hill Lord Vulcan still distill his spam,
so please do exhale that cancer crap far out

on its way." /
                V and the teen conspired in giggles.
"Abby's my name." /
                     Said V: "I have four female friends
I'd like you, Abby, to join and meet. They wriggle
their redhead charms, they shout out alarms to give males bends,

just same as you." V pulled a brooch from her crimson purse
and pinned it on the girl's left breast. "Woodhull for Prez!"
it read. /
            The girl said, "You?" /
                     V blew smoke, somber as a hearse.
"Just want you to know," the teen said, "I'm not no lez."

Vickie remembered Doc Eddie. "We can't all have luck
in drawing of our genes." /
                     The springy teen did laugh. /
"They're at the Civic Center now. Go on and shuck.
Four redheads. You'll see." /
                     The teen romped off; Alonzo gave chaff,

"You be sending that bouncy around Judge Roy Bean?" /
"Herself she can take care of. I have great faith.
But you and I, sweet friend, need to stay lean
and follow that Hoover guy. He's a foul wraith,

"of that I stay certain." /
                     "What about your godpop?" /
"My what? Oh, Dio . . . yes, him we also need to bring.
No telling what trouble he and his lantern might drop
on souls naive." Vickie gave fast screech as her purse made ring.

Lonz, gentleman pure, inquired, "May I?" When V
sent nervous nod, he opened her purse. A crimson iPhone
did vibrate and sing. Alonzo looked to see
caller i.d. "Say it from Diogenes." /
                     V gave moan;

Alonzo pressed Answer. The speaker woofed two great howls
and then, "Vickie, 'Tis I. And Pluto. We're walking out.
I see you two. Keep him there. He's The One, my bowels
they tell me that. All these poor firemen were a rout." /

"What a marvel," V said, eyeing the crimson cell.
She pictured her England time, its snaky black phones.
So clothing was not the only thing that turned out swell.
But, "nigger?" Social grace sure hadn't honed

itself as well. *Go catch that slag*, an inner voice rang.
Him and his lecher friend. Then things up here will move quite well.
Such voices, V knew, often bust. But she didn't complain.
Giving dust to Violet Toes and that judge would sure feel swell.

Was then she spied D and Pluto sneaking toward Alonzo.
Their inner voices held no doubts: Mocha was The One.
In joy, D thrust his lantern, dancing, going gonzo . . .
No flame. No fuel. No test. D slumped a hellish slump.

Perceiving the problem, V rushed to rub D's neck,
while Pluto licked his master's skinny ankles.
"Oh man," Lonz said. "Lantern dead. Nearest propane's a trek."
These words brought gushing tears to D, not rankles.

"Gotta go," he yelped. "I'll be right back." /
                                            V offered a kiss,
an act she'd never dared when she thought him Demosthenes.
But ol' sleep-in-a-jug deserved some bliss.
She looked from him to Lonz, whom she would often please,

had she half a chance to share love's hot wheeze.

Chapter Fourteen: A Fuel-up in Hades

Wherein Diogenes refuels his lantern, makes complaint, receives reply.

Dio stood in line at the Central Fueling Station.
Always a line formed at the station. Why? What use
could Folk make of slush refined from Styx? Oblations
to soothe Lord Hades? Why? He'd just dole more abuse.

Dio grabbed Pluto's collar, thinking Cerberus would
be guarding the pump. But no, it was Hades himself:
"Sure hope you didn't run out just before your lantern could
locate The One. Might be that guy with the lady's thin self."

Lord Hades gave a slimeball grin. "Got your i. d.?" /
"You know who I am! Twenty-four hundred years!" /
"Rules are rules. I don't make them." /
                                    "No? Who does? Heidi?" /
D fumbled with his crimson billfold. Twelve hundred seers

down here, and not a one could change Lord Hades' mean foul ways. /
"You know," Hades said, inspecting Dio's proffered card,
"on the side of that lantern there's a tiny fuel gauge." /
D sizzled as if dropped in a skillet of hot lard.

"Just fill it. I'm in a rush." /
                            "Where're you sleeping? Motel 6?
Want me to send up a wine jug?" /
                            Hades, the clown,
would it ever change? "Your attitude could use a fix." /
"Really? Mayhap those sandals are dragging you down.

"Here's a new pair. Bonus points with your fill-up.
See? My attitude works fine. Needs encouragement, that's all." /
Dio donned them with regret. If his arches were still up
one hour from now, a wonder. Hades' face took on pall:

"You better scoot back. Your gal's in trouble at some mall."

Chapter Fifteen: Disappointment at the Civic Center

After being misdirected by Hades, Diogenes finds Victoria at the Civic Center. News that the rock concert has been cancelled sends the surrounding teens into sudden dismay. The Judge and J. Edgar offer to transport five teenage girls to Five Points, where the Judge, on seeing Frank Fleming's controversial Storyteller, known to locals as "Bob," is inspired to display his own sculpture in the middle of every Alabama town. Victoria, seeing the same sculptured fountain, momentarily fears a bad omen. Then she espies the owl perched on the Storyteller's staff and becomes assured. J Edgar, meanwhile, espies the Five Furies dipping in the fountain and becomes certain he's uncovered a communist cell.

It cost Pluto and D one hour from Hades' misdirect.
Of course Dame V was at no mall, but tracing down Hoover
and newfound pal, the king of child abuse elect.
Those two had stayed at the Civic Center, future movers

of youth's bright cheer. At least, thus thought Roy Bean.
J Ed kept not so sure. He feared civil unrest
impending perched. These screams and laughs—what other could they
      mean?
For his tommy gun he searched, or a pistol in his vest.

But naught. How quell the commies sans bullets and guns?
Just where were his? And just where was he, these last many years?
He thought today was his birthday: some gifts would be fun,
but would these kids deliver? Likely not, he feared.

Birmingham, was it? A field office sat down here;
he'd call, remind 'em of his birthday, get agents
to scurry, plus assess this insurrection blooming near.
The key to quelling lay in prudence, for all events.

Put 'em down, lock 'em up. With those Civil Rights folk,
he'd done as much, as best he could, to hamstring them.
That impure M. L. King, slippery as egg yolk;
And Mother Jones—he'd sent her on a Gulfstream swim

to Russia. See how you like it there, you foul wench.
Yes, keeping the U. S. commie-free took a ready touch.
From what recent he'd seen, indifference formed a cinch,
was pulling tight. The Reds would sneak back in and muck

dear Uncle Sam if common folk fell to commie cells
increasing like a cancer, horrid and fast.

"Red commies!" he blurted. "The Bureau will stop their swell!"
Yes, he'd phone there now, warn of the toppling mast

occurring here. Act fast, to last. He tugged his billfold.
Virgin white with a whore red A? What confabulation
brought this about? /
                 "Hey pops! I'm for Auburn! Mold Tide, mold!" /
J. Ed blinked. This young set was a tribulation

to be endured, he supposed. "Is there a phone nearby?" /
"What, your battery gone dead?" The boy pointed to
the cell phone in J. Ed's pocket. J. Ed gave it the eye. /
"Here, use mine. 'Slong as you don't call Saban. He's jointed to

the Devil. Saban means Satan my momma says."
J. Ed stared blankly at the phone. "Geesh," the boy groaned. "Old folks.
Here, want me to call for you too?" /
                 "Crime doesn't pay,"
J. Ed advised, feeling chummy. "It only stokes

"discontent and commies." /
                 "What are commies?" asked the lad. /
"Phone the local FBI and there you'll learn."
Or burn, J. Ed wanted to add. But on the gad
a wail arose from all about, sounding harsh, sounding stern.

"The concert's cancelled! The electric just zonked out!" /
The teens stood stunned, their faces lumped in goldfish stares.
World Death, did it lie near? Judge Bean Too, he looked about:
this offered the perfect chance—these shoulders so bare,

these girlies forlorn. He spied one wearing a brooch.
Old-fashioned, just ready for judicial charms.
"All's not lost," he told her, working his lips in smooch.
"Starbucks at Five Points's not bought the electric farm.

"You need a lift there?" /
                 "Got room for my four girlfriends?" /
The judge looked to four redheads. *My God, my God,*
he thought, *Thy bounty comes swift, it never ends.*
He gave his boots a wag, to show himself well shod.

V's four Furies, plus one, they scoffed those shiny boots,
cast beady eyes at the beady-eyed judge: "Just take us, Pops."

The judge, he feared his case might turn moot,
but then, a creep's hope doth always give spring and hop,

so he performed a manly bow and gesture,
then led J. Ed and five swell teens toward his pick-up truck,
envisioning the just parade they made: "Rest your-
selves in my bed." He gave a wink and pluck

at one red-head's soft bare shoulder. Together all four hissed.
Roy Bean just laughed. "A well-respected judge, that's me, you know." /
The fifth girl, named Abby, lent him a judicial tongue kiss.
"And you, old man," she asked J. Ed. "Enjoy the show?" /

V stood nearby. She gave grim grin at Lonzo:
"See? Wisely I chose. They're all hot into
taking care, belaying any rank male show.
They'll have that pervert-o slick judge hopping to

their will." /
             Alonzo, like J. Ed, stayed uncertain.
This judge had a rep, and that Hoover fellow, well,
the combo seemed able to sling down the curtain.
"We need to follow them, yes? See what type of hell

"gets played." /
             So they sneaked by as Judge Bean twisted his key
and sniffed perfume that bent his mind like junior prom.
Abby, she twisted to tug the cab's rear window in glee.
A Fury peeked in; upon the judge did she glom;

"Come on," she urged, "Pop it! Let's move it to see Bob,
the only male I'll trust." /
             "He's not a commie,
is he?" /
      "What's a commie?" /
             J. Ed let out a sob.
Could it really be true? These kids, straight from Mommy,

knew not the world's most slimèd evil, most foul oppressor?
And who was this fellow named Bob, if not a Red?
After that Kennedy creep, brother two successor,
became Attorney General, that name vexed J. Ed.

Bob, Ob, Bo Bob, Banana Anna, Bo Bob—
the song went thus, and thus the foul name rang.

A redhead reached through the window to tug his fob,
"What's this, old man? You wrap your penis in a chain?" /

J. Ed sputtered; the judge stepped on the gas,
supposing himself surrounded by five hot teens.
The Indigo Hotel down there held loads of class.
He could impress these five while J. Ed spent spleen

on searching out commies. /
                      "Whee!" the four in back
yelled as he slid through a corner. *Speed on*. The cops were all
back at the Center, quelling a teen riot on track
to bring the city down. Too bad ol' Bull couldn't haul

some good Christian dogs and fire hoses
in to settle matters. The judge slowed to street park;
the four redheads blossomed like four roses
to quit the truck's rust bed. Brunette Abby showed snark,

and called out, "Run! Flick your panties, give the oldsters a thrill!"
Crimson, violet, pink, rose, and black their panties showed.
Judge Bean Too and J. Ed turned red, their sublime wills
providing different reasons for that fiery glow.

From their car, Alonzo and V observed.
"Sure learn fast," Lonz commented. "Let's follow and watch." /
"They'll give that slime ball judge just what he deserves,"
V asserted. "Still, we *should* stop, make certain there's no botch."

Alonzo parked. The day'd turned torrid, deep South hot;
so much that even a cop's cop would shun java.
Alonzo picked the perfect illegal parking spot.
They followed J. Ed, the judge, and the teenage lava,

who still jumped and hopped, showing multicolored panties.
V grabbed Alonzo's arm. "Reminds me of my sister." /
"Where she at?" /
                  "Oh, back home with her aunties.
Besides, don't you flit in interest, mister!" /

Alonzo grinned. "That we learn when I meet her.
A jealous pinch get your bad self in blister?"
Again, he grinned. /
                "Sweet sir, two can toss life into blur.
What say I turn lez and tempt all three *your* sisters?"

The both of them gave laugh. Alonzo popped a high-five,
which V figured to return. Their palms tingled
in magic, wouldn't you know? Such happens when you're alive.
V blinked. A crowd nearby did mull. She mingled.

A cast bronze vision like she'd never seen glistening
in Hades gave show: The Storyteller Fountain splashed.
A ram's head man, book in hand—before him, listening,
perched turtles and rabbits enraptured, unabashed.

About them, her five Furies danced happy circles
to wade cool water in the fountain. V's body stiffened:
the ram's head man also held a staff with aura purple . . .
an owl, though, perched atop the staff! Her heart quickened

at that good omen. Surely this go-round would work right!
No Comstock, no Beecher! Wisdom would prevail!
Doc Eddie then, waving a finger, burst into her sight.
Beside him, Diogenes and Pluto let out their wails.

"Your godfather's quite the character," Lonz observed. /
"My—" Remembering her white lie, V replied,
"That's why my mom appointed him." Lies played absurd,
the tangles they lent. But truth, alas, got you fried.

Consider Beecher preacher porking parishioners.
Enough. She observed: Dio and Doc stood to the fore
to watch the Furies cavort like commissioners
collecting tax. /
              "Those five be dancing their own lore

"at Storyteller Fountain." /
                 "So why does a ram
sit reading from a book, with an owl on his staff?" /
"Street folk nomenclate him Bob. He be gentle like a lamb.
Bronzed creatures in the pond be spellbound with his gaff.

"Kept me la same when me and my three sis' saw Ram-man,
with Pop and Mom telling he weren't no voodoo laugh."
Alonzo told of sculptor Frank Fleming's plan
to show the story-telling South, but how white riff-raff

became dead certain the fountain held Satan.
Meanwhile, the Five furies, they danced. Several young men
had gathered to clap, no doubt thinking of mating.
Forever thus doth warble this globe's long-sung blend,

which surely beats those hard-flung chants at the Civic Center.
As multi-colored panties showed, the Judge broke sweat.
J. Ed, meanwhile, took out cards on which he did enter
abundant notes, all concerning the commie threat,

especially from that mocha fellow who sneaked
his arm around that unsuspecting Northern lass.
Clapping, dancing, laughing, and singing leaked
throughout the street.
                    One of life's sad edicts is, *All must pass.*

It did. One Fury gave tumble. She fell against
an enthralled bronze rabbit, astride an enthralled bronze turtle.
Doc Eddie waded in as the frightened crowd winced.
"I'm a doctor!" he cried. "Give way!" He hurtled

toward the bleeding Fury to prop her head;
he hurtled to his car and back in supernatural time;
he hurtled swabs and tetanus shot before you could have said
"Jim Dandy, how handy!" (Doc's car held no such rhyme,

but everything else, it seemed.) He gave the Fury a pat,
then distributed almond dark chocolate from a sack.
Meantime, the Judge, he looked at the blood and—kersplat!—
envisioned a virgin, lying on her back.

J Ed looked too. Her blood was Red. It gave his hip a whack.

Chapter Sixteen: Nightfall,
or Nothing Good Happens After Ten, Exhibit A

With oncoming night, those concerned split into three groups. Herein, Alonzo and Victoria head for Alonzo's apartment, followed by the four now five Furies who woo an Uber cabbie into tailing their new idol, Victoria.

The weightlifter Charles Atlas said it first:
"Nothing good happens after ten p.m."
Oh Charles, we all do fear your life the worse
for that prudish ditty, filled not with wisdom, but b.m.

As if to prove you wrong, from over the Atlantic Sea
did float Arnold, partier, lifter, governor deluxe.
Just thus did float Alonzo and Vickie, fillèd with glee,
to Lonz's car, crammed not with teens like Judge Bean's truck,

nor with mysteries, like Doc Eddie's Town Car—
but yet, when Lonz's hand ground that four-on-the-floor,
it shifted V into high amour, and a star
pulsed hotly in her below, as she clung unto the door.

For relief she glanced at the side mirror and spotted
her Furies five piling into a crimson car.
She smiled. Work not too shoddy for time allotted.
One turn. Two. Then three. Behind, never off too far,

the crimson stayed. Good to have a faithful department,
V thought, but even better to have a mocha man.
Soon enough they reached Alonzo's apartment,
a second-story with a New Orleans balcony plan.

"Lovely," V said, stepping inside, though Lonz's taste
in art did lean toward Haiti's voodoo side.
"Such a fine cool night, 'twould be a barren waste
not to leave that balcony door open wide.

"Lady moon gives our earthly love more ardor,
the man in her grins with each terrene embrace.
Together, they fill our temporal larder
with caritas, to shove hatred out on its face."

V dropped her pose and purse, flipped off her green sandals,
once more amazed by modernity's loose attire.

Meanwhile below, the Furies five, acting as vandals,
formed a cheerleader's pyramid to take them higher

right onto that New Orleans balcony, where they perched
and waited, stowing giggles, opening baby doll eyes
to watch and learn and hear.
                              Their wait proved worth
the time—'twas not too long. The five stifled their sighs.

Was just as well the Uber guy, who'd fallen in lust,
had driven off. The show he would have seen!
V's insidest part grew moist; Lonz's stick perched to bust.
Their tossing grew hot; their tossing stayed lean.

Warm cozy bats will cling to moist cave walls;
rabbits will burrow deep in earthly dens;
squirrels will chitter and frolic, collecting nuts in fall;
silken foxes will amble o'er verdant glens—

thus nature provideth example galore.
Are we not to follow? Are we, like Charles Atlas,
meant to hit a solitary sack and snore?
To lock our front doors, wailing, 'Home, safe at last'?

No! Ten wide eyes espied The Way in Lonz's apartment,
where Vickie, enflamed to have her body young again,
coaxed Lonz, stout envoy from the police department,
into committing lusts high unto his carnal chin.

La, the sounds they created: "Ahh," "whee," "more," "please-please."
"Harder." "Faster." "Slower." "Longer." "Linger-linger."
They turned and churned, creating a flip-flop trapeze
of mocha-ivory, ivory-mocha. A single singer,

they changed that B'ham apartment into a universe
where lush galaxies spiraled soundlessly,
planets rotated, suns were born, then burst,
hydrogen joined oxygen to sprinkle boundlessly.

They gave life sweet meaning, they gave it moan.
Yes, the affirmation came: *this* is what we give for,
this cancels ditches and pratfalls, *this* is the loam,
what every human—nay, every creature—lives for.

The Furies looked on, enwrapped in silence
until one whispered, "So that's how it's done!"
Continuing to watch the tossing, peaceful violence
they studied how this sad world might be won.

And thus Vickie's Free-Love platform united, momently,
black and white, male and female, old and young—even the bugs
that crawled in cupboards and twitched out coos. Listen intently:
if B'ham—the universe!—might consist only of hugs,

perhaps there really might be a benevolent
creator sitting on some happy cedar swing,
with his—or her!—breath easing out, redolent
of patchouli and birds and bees on the wing.

Five wide-eyed youthful spies, believing thus, began to sing.

Chapter Seventeen: Nightfall, or Nothing Good Happens After Ten, Exhibit B

J. Edgar Hoover and Judge Roy Bean Too remain at the Storyteller Fountain, awaiting the inspiration they confidently expect to arrive. In this Exhibit, it seems Mr. Atlas was correct in his affirmation.

In kindness let us suppose no one is always wrong—
nor always right, we fear! Just so, that weightlifter guy,
Chuck Atlas, surely might heft a mind-muscle sometimes strong.
Indeed, while gazing on Judge Bean still skulking by

the moonlit Storyteller Fountain, we respect Chuck's truth:
oh nothing, nothing good stirs likely to occur.
The Judge, by the bye, in his demented youth
read a comic book—that Satanic burr,

according to his Baptist grampypap—and therein saw
an ad encouraging spindly youth to take up
barbells so they might beat every bully raw.
Yes, this from that same Atlas fellow, wanting to shake up

American scrawn and send them roaring forth
(before 10 p.m. only!) to take back beaches and parks
from bullies kicking sand. What grand paranoid girth
Chuck did impart! Judge Bean Too took it all to heart:

Hie thee to law school and get thee degreed;
hie thee courtward, be it legal or in a mall;
hie thee unto power, mark the globe with thine pee;
in the Good Lord's name, hie thee, and never crawl!

Thus teenage girlies will flock unto thine biblical arms!
So, as he watched the Satanic Storyteller ram-man—
a vision came! Alabama town squares would pulse alarms,
fifteen-tons of Commandments Ten, a ham-stand

to spin the South! He turned to J. Ed,
to outline his plan. /
                    "Roy, they won't allow statued
teenage girlies, especially naked and unwed,"
J. Ed replied in paternal platitude. /

For one passing moment, Judge Bean did envision
teen girls in bras and panties holding the tablets
two, but lust petered, and as his hormones wizened,
his righteous side unfurled. "No. In every hamlet

"a bearded God will settle his kind, white hand.
He will select, then calm misguided souls.
And if they don't obey and pacify the land,
He'll throttle hell from them, until they get enrolled." /

J. Ed smiled admiringly at his newfound friend.
"Just one thing I'd add to your admirable plan:
omni-directional bugs—to assure God's end!—
we'll wire into those fine tablets. Yes, I too see them stand

"strong, to unify this breadbasket land. Good people
fear not what they say, but intellectuals and commies
will justly be punished by our all-hearing steeple—" /
"Yay!" Judge Bean exclaimed. "Ring their little tommys!" /

J Ed winced. He saw a world led by righteous mommies.

Chapter Eighteen: Nightfall,
or Nothing Good Happens After Ten, Exhibit C

Diogenes, Pluto, and Doc Eddie depart in Doc Eddie's spacious Lincoln Town Car, the trunk of which holds a warehouse of goods. This last Exhibit leaves us where we started and remain quite likely to stay: that is, uncertain, which is exactly what Doc Eddie's FMRI concludes.

Oh Chuck, the jury sits hung. Were you right, or just a bum?
V and Alonzo compacted in soulful love;
J Ed and Judge, they whirled out hatred's hum.
Might our third post-ten option settle witness from above?

More like from below, for Hades is making shove
to be heard. "C'mon," Doc Eddie pleaded,
"I've got a portable FMRI in my spacious glove
compartment. I'll inject the dye while you're seated.

"Just a little burn is all you'll feel." /
                                    "Used to that,"
Diogenes replied. "Aren't we, fellow?" Pluto
gave whine. /
                    "You're a sport." The doc injected juice to splat
Dio's veins. D gave frazzle, his body made like Newto-

nian mechanics had foraken it. 'Twas then Albert
Einstein stepped in. D's torso gave quiver. Pluto nudged
his hand. /
                    "Gotta stay still," the Doc warned. "No overt
movement." Pluto bared teeth and growled. Doc Eddie judged

he'd better placate this hound from Lord Hades' hell,
so two old Trump steaks he pried from his freezer
to pop in the Town Car's microwave. Just as well
he'd refused to eat them, for he was no believer

in Make Sure America Ate Again.
The dog gave gnaw while the FMRI whirred.
Doc Eddie studied the results and gave grand grin.
"I knew it! I knew it! My machine has concurred!

"Dead folk don't know one flit more than we living do!" /
Dio, still woozy from the dye, hoisted his lantern high.
"You joke. You need machines to tell you that? Cows moo,
blowflies shoo, but dead or alive, humans only can sigh."

D watched his lantern sputter as it neared *his* face,
remindful that he too played no honest man.
He thought of Vickie, no doubt at the mocha guy's place.
"Wait. We *can* hug and kiss and screw, which makes things grand.

I guess that's *one* good thing humans might do." /
Doc Eddie stopped his skipping about on the street.
He pondered what the old gent just said. "Yes, making woo
presents a worthy alternative. It sure beats

chasing 'commies,' hating 'niggers,' 'crackers,' or 'queers,'
rousting up dead ideas to lend plain misery
to those alive. Better off wooing and drinking beers."
He paused. "And supping micro-brewery delivery

of the latter shows impeccable taste." The Doc
stowed his FMRI machine, then turned to celebrate.
"Imagine! Dead or alive, either flock
holds not a damned bit more wisdom. That's great!" /

"No, it grates," Dio intoned. "Don't suppose you've got
some wine in that fulsome car? Pinot noir would fit
the mood to perfection. Bitter, dark, and served snot-hot." /
"Well of course. A good jug will belay your snit,"

Doc Eddie replied. /
                    That fine word "jug"
did send alarm through Diogenes. Was getting late,
where might he sleep? He'd really like to plug
his tired body into . . . "Say, by any sort of fate

"would that spacious car of yours encase a
large wine jug? 'Swhat I'm used to sleeping in, you know.
I'd rather its solitary confines than face a
pack of lying hounds—no offense, pooch, don't grow

"angry." /
          "He's using metaphor," the Doc added
helpfully. Pluto didn't respond. He'd just begun
his second Trump Steak, and he'd padded
off a bit from interfering human types. Let them run

their mouths endlessly; his jaws had grinding
to activate. /
              "To answer your query, let me look."

61

Doc Eddie pulled out a bottle of pinot noir, finding
a corkscrew under his seat. Beside it lay a book,

some trash called *Pineapple* Homeless Lena'd given him
after a nighttime drive to the local Y.
Wait! In his trunk, in the back, hard driven in
amongst ten packs of Ziploc diapers . . . "Oh my!"

Doc Eddie shouted. "Wine, corkscrew and a great big jug!
This night has been kind." /
                              "Really? You have one?" /
"One? I have two! I'll join you! Pluto will keep away thugs."
Doc Eddie thought camping out had always been such fun.

They sipped Pinot, Pluto gnawed—good after ten, had it won?

Chapter Nineteen: Dawn. Will Something Good Happen After Eight?

After an indecisive night, insofar as Charles Atlas's maxim, we find the Five Furies awakening Alonzo and Vickie. Together, all seven depart toward a commotion at the Storyteller Fountain, on a tip from Alonzo's police scanner and scads of videos from the iPhones of the Furies.

"La-la. La-la laaaa luh-la-la. La-la laaaa luh-la-la
Laaaaaa laa la." /

        Really? Lonz thought. *Leonard Cohen?*
He'd been clasping Vickie's left breast and dreaming fa-la's
but was awakened by this female chorus blowing

a tune from his balcony. They bounced like five
ninjas; they sang like five angels. Get his gun or a cross?
Vickie awoke. "Aww, look. Aren't they sweet? A hive
of princess bees to watch us as we toss." /

"You bumped a lot the while," the Fury Abby said. /
White folk weirdness, Lonzo thought. But remembering
how he'd spied on his sisters three in baths and bed
he fast forsook his racial dismembering.

Was just as well, since his police scanner blasted
10-20's, -40's, and other arcane lore.
"What's it mean?" Vickie asked. /

        "Those two nuts outlasted
us at Bob's fountain. They're spreading thwarting hatred gore,"

a Fury replied, displaying her iPhone,
a chalice clasping the spirit-key to life's tired puzzle.
V recalled she had a crimson one on loan
from Hades, which fact sent no transcendent nuzzle.

The scanner squawked more Arabic numerals out,
as if colluding in jihad. "Better get on down."
Alonzo said. "We can stop at Wendy's for a bout
of coffee and sausage." /

        "Chocolate Frosties!" That gave resound

from the balcony. /
        "This Wendy, is she your sis?"
V asked, though shamed by sudden jealousy,

for what good free love, if not free to spread its bliss?
Is not this why she rose from Hades, to rouse, to see

if earth's torrid hatred could be hurled far out?
She started from the bed. /
                              "Please," Lonzo intoned,
"Could you five turn your heads?"
                              Though the furies gave shout,
they did comply. Uplifting pastel iPhones,

they hunched like monkeys five, figures to make Darwin happy. /
"So. Just how *did* you get here?" V asked when they packed
in Lonz's car. *Red? Wasn't it white? Or was she sappy?*
"Uber," one Fury replied.
                              Another god? V racked

her brain, but 'twas no use. She smiled at the five
atop one another, comfy in the car's back seat.
More numbers spewed from Lonz's two-way. "A whole tribe
is dancing at the Fountain." /
                              The furies gave bleat:

"Chocolate Frosties, remember! Those oldsters can wait!" /
Alonzo complied, for he had a caffeine head . . .
But Homeless Lena sat guard at the drive-thru's lane. "Too late,"
she chirped, as in her coffee a tenth sugar pack she fed.

"They closed because of the do at the Bob Fountain.
I'm keeping guard. The owner lent me this coffee
and egg sandwich to watch." /
                              Her news caused pouting
of six, though V, filled with love's mocha and toffee,

endured no gastric remiss. /
                              "Durp. Hot Dog Rita
will be down there. I'd go with, but I gotta watch
this lane. Rita sells ice cream, coffee, and dogs to feed a
city twice the size of 'Ham. Your hunger she'll scotch.

"Durp. Either that or make you drop." Homeless Lena
gave a homeless grin and plopped one more sugar packet in.
Her coffee, already granular enough to clean a
switchblade of rust, weaved like sociopathic sin.

Two cats appeared from behind Wendy's far wall.
When Lena split her sandwich, each hissed at each.
"No, no, you'll set bad example by spreading gall!
How will humans ever learn, durp, if you don't teach?"

She spryly jumped and opened four creamers
two for each. /
              "Aww, look. She's being so sweet,"
Abby said. /
             Lonz slit his eyes, thinking, *Dreamer!*
But best keep mum, not his place to set this child on her feet.

Something about weird Lena made his shoulder jerk.
Was an inborn tic he respected. Like voodoo
it worked, who knew why? No other cop dared to smirk;
but gave long listen if his shoulder danced hoodoo

against some seeming quiet, gentle gal or guy,
no matter if they were black, brown, yellow, or white—
Lonz's tics were famous for not letting a creep get by.
Was claimed, in fact, his tics could cure B'ham's crime blight.

With a last look at Lena and her scrawny cats,
Alonzo shoved his car in gear, sneaking a touch
to Vickie's knee. /
             "Oh stop it," Abby spat.
"Wasn't last night enough? /
                   "Too much be never too much!"

Alonzo replied. The Furies began to sing,
so Vickie clapped and Lonzo beat the steering wheel.
"Oh look!" Abby cried. Left, then right, she gave fling
to playing cards she'd found. Even the jokers smiled for real.

. . . Such happiness could not last: they neared Bob's fountain,
where hatred's apothegms were stomping out mean reels.
While joy had grown in the car, here odium was mounting.
The city's morning air wavered. There came a squeal.

"Must be a party!" V exclaimed. "Let's join!"
Beside V's head Abby thrust to point out the Judge.
"Don't think so," Lonz replied. "That guy have a groin
that mash different than most." /
                   "And we have a grudge

"to settle with him," Abby hissed. /
                              "The hot dog
lady!" One Fury gave shout. Hate, belly? Belly, hate?
While V stayed placid with love, hatred's flog
made jangles insistent. Is such our lasting human fate?

McDonald's doth try to sate our bellies,
Pizza Hut and Hardees give it a whir,
but evil orange gremlins flood our tellies,
tossing calm and caritas far off in a blur.

The Furies piled from Lonz's car, as neat as they'd piled in.
"Be polite for five minutes," V admonished. /
"Polite is as polite does." They pointed. The Judge, riled in
some theocratic penile weave, astonished

the crowd by flapping his arms as if to levitate.
"A monument of hard granite in every 'Bama town!
We'll lead this country from sin, we'll gravitate
toward The Way. No more unnatural wedding gowns!"

A cheer arose. "Let America hate again!"
The Judge smiled; J Ed took copious notes,
observing about. Spotting Mocha Man, he focused in. /
"Friends," the Judge yelped. "We sail a sinking boat!

"Affirm now we must! I'm proud to carry a gun
in my holster. Jesus scattered the Pharisees
and moneylenders. With an AR-15 they'd have run
whole lots faster!" /
                              Cheers arose, feet clomped in glee.

"The first we'll erect is in the Capitol,
right by Ol' Johnny Reb's historic White House.
Oh but that House swept white and pure. The slap it all
took laid us low. The time has come to roar, to rouse

America to—"
                              "Let America hate again!"
That cheer took flight. Enough feet stomped so's the water
in Storyteller Fountain sloshed. Bronzed frogs gave spin,
as if in fear of amphibian slaughter.

The Furies had endured their five-minute
politeness span. They enjoined arms to chant,
"Make fug, not war!" Not even one live minute
passed. The four farm boys from before started to rant.

They faced off. J Ed took notes; the judge hid his lust-lump;
Vickie climbed the fountain, Lonz patted his gun;
Diogenes showed; his lantern sputtered dust thumps;
Pluto howled dismay; Doc Eddie's slow machine couldn't run

fast enough to plot. Hot Dog Rita? She alone had fun.

Chapter Twenty: A Plea to Hades

Diogenes and Pluto travel back to Hades to query the Lord's motives and refuel preventatively, since the lantern had gotten a workout by Bob's Fountain.

Lord Hades was munching a Pop-Tart when
Pluto and Diogenes appeared. He tossed the Tart
to Pluto, whose jaws snapped and gave a spin.
"No," Hades tutored. "Not that type of tart, it has no heart

to break. —My jokes grow weak." /
                                  This guy's getting all the puns,
Dio moaned. *I'm left with sticks in the Styx.*
Lord Zeus knows I've given that one too many runs.
"Pluto and me were wondering . . . something you might fix—" /

"Sure, sure. Anything for you two. So how's Aboveworld?
I saw you acquired two jugs and a friend." /
"A smart neurologist. He's discovered logic mis-twirls
the same if you're quick or you're dead."
                                That note did send

a burst of laughter from Hades and Dio both. /
"Need some fuel? Self-service to keep up with the times."
When D cocked a brow, Hades said, "Today I'm into sloth.
Tomorrow though, I'll install hourly Baptist church chimes." /

"Don't think they like them, too close to a Pope.
Say, I've just got to ask: That J Ed weirdo is tossing
glass shards enough. But the Judge fellow . . . I'm losing hope." /
Lord Hades heard a ding. "His distribution's Gaussian." /

Confused, Pluto and D shook their heads. /
                                   "The normal
amount of idiots is what the Judge and his fans
present." The Lord opened his microwave, gave a formal
bow. "Such shouldn't make Vickie abandon her plans.

"—Pshaw, berry flavored." The Lord frowned at the tart in his hand.

Chapter Twenty-one: Plans Get Formed

Two weeks pass. The Judge is raising money to erect the first of the granite monuments in Montgomery, promising he will place one in every incorporated town in Alabama. Vickie is enrolling more Furies.

"Ten minutes." /
           "That's six hundred one-Mississippi's!" /
"As vanguards of Free Love In Peace, you'll need your math."
By their eye-rolls V saw her words left them drippy;
yet they formed two silent lines, through which she made her path.

"Make fug not war," one Fury hissed. V put a finger
to her lips. "Ten minutes. Just listen and stand." /
The Judge stood ranting his spiel. Like a stinger
it jerked a mostly white crowd to demand:

"Bring back the good ol' days!" Four farm boys hopped
and spat tobacco. Women clutched crimson purses
unto their love organs while the farm boys flopped.
Nearby, twelve white-cloaked doctors and nurses

gave guard to a sacred square. "Our country needs a flu shot!
It needs some swine vaccination. Humanists are creeping
about to chew its base. God's granite, that will crush their rot!"
The judge spun a blued gun from his holster. This sent leaping

and moans through the mass.
           "Thirty-eight Mississippi's,"
the Furies simpered.
           Dio worked the crowd.
His lantern registered just like it once had with hippies
who shrilled their righteous screech, and so many more in time's shroud:

Maoists, Nazis—all fascists of yore. /
           Pluto sniffed
a dropped hot dog—botulous, despite its sodium.
But wait! Might it be laced with poison spliff?
A toddler bent. Pluto snatched the dog of odium

and scarfed it. Though he couldn't die twice,
his stomach at once tossed bilious and sick.
The toddler gave an angry cry, so ridden with lice
that Pluto almost mourned not leaving the poisonous stick.

Would not this tot be better off beneath the ground?
Set free from scabies, hunger, child abuse?
But then, might he not turn his life around?
Hawking won the Nobel, made himself of great use.

But Gacy and Dahmer grew as children abused.
What good ever came from them? *Still, I am my
master's lifelong friend. His ways have loosed
themselves on me: no human pup should ever die.*

Homeless Lena stood nearby. She pushed a small cart.
How ever did she get from 'Ham to Montgomery? /
Dio, hearing the tot's cry, practiced lantern art:
a no-go, of course. The kid opened his mouth in a plea.

At least his hunger stays honest enough, Dio thought.
Homeless Lena trundled her cart. Dio waved,
remembering the helpful misspelled sign she'd wrought.
She gave the toddler a hot dog, which stopped his raves.

A shill? Dio gave a rueful laugh. It would never end.
He looked about. The Furies counting their Mississippis
until the moment they might let loose and upend
the Judge, himself preaching Gospel while sneaking lips' ease

from teenage girls, like the Beecher Preacher Creature,
dazzling female parishioners with Jesus
while inserting his penis, his true main feature—
all that we humans do, in end, seems done just to please us.

Plato and his boys, Hitler and his Jews,
Mao and intellectuals, Calvin and power,
this Hoover fellow judging Civil Rights a ruse
for Red Scare Commies. Pelosi and Trump glower

until their goals get subsumed. Doc Eddie's machine—
for sure it exhibits the Final Truth: that Way
lies brambly, cluttered with Nietzsche's mind vipers lean.
Of course. No human on course ever knew, where that course lay.

Dio watched Pluto trailing after Lena,
wagging his tail for a dog. *A good enough pun.
Well, dogs stay honest. Though that doesn't mean a
whole lot. I could hardly make them my lantern's run.*

A mother walked by, searching out her toddler.
Half-heartedly, Dio held his lantern up. It made fizz. /
"This will be the first of many," the Judge, no coddler
of any, cried out. "In every town! We mean biz-

"ness!"
       "Let America hate again!" the crowd replied.
Victoria raised her soft and loving palm.
"Make fug, not war!" Her furies shouted out high.
Dio sighed. He should have been a beggar of alms,

kept expectations low, Siddhartha by the river,
there watching time amass—just like failed lantern quests.
Of sudden, straight through Dio passed a cold quiver:
What about that Alonzo cop? The for-real test?

Now where the hell was Pluto? Good mental news
arrives and he's off with a shill. A lantern test
awaits, my boy! Let us see if that detective's shoes
can skip another lantern swing. Hope still rests!

"Awoo!" D howled. Pluto stayed gone, playing close to the vest.

Chapter Twenty-two: J Ed Contacts the Field Office

J Ed demands, without success, that the Birmingham field office send him a present. In consequence, he questions the patriotic status of the South.

J Ed caressed the iPhone in his pocket,
remembering the kid whose mom was a Saban hater.
Did she support commies deep in her breast locket?
Was this Saban fella a ruse? Was he a baiter?

The kid had shown him how to call the FBI;
the Judge had Googled the field office many times.
A handsome three stories white, it gave the South the lie.
I'll call there now, I'll ring their wayward chimes!

"You have reached the Birmingham Office—" /
                                  "J Edgar Hoover
here. Connect me to the—" /
                      "—of the FBI. If—" /
"I want your boss, lady. And hurry, move or—" /
"If this is an emergency hang up quick—" /

"You missed my birthday! That's emergency enough." /
"—and dial 911. If you are a law officer—" /
"I don't want no local boys involved. We're rough, tough
enough." /
         "Please press 1." /
                        "My birthday! This office sure

"is a mess. Give me Johnnie. He's still here, yes?" /
"If you are seeking employment as an agent—" /
"Lady, how you operate here is anyone's guess.
Give me Johnnie or—" inspiration!—"I'll send Saban!" /

"If you would like to hear these options again . . ." /
J Ed grimaced. The South was the very last place
where he thought commies would infiltrate and win.
The Judge was right; they ran in a desperate race.

Could that mom be right? Saban and Satan glowed the same face?

Chapter Twenty-three: Alonzo Uncovers a Trend

Detective Alonzo Rankin, while sifting his paperwork, notices an anomaly, which alerts him to possible misdeeds. He plans to meet with Victoria at the famed statue of Vulcan on Red Mountain to observe a political rally pertaining to J Ed and The Judge.

The piles of paper were strewn endless; the computer's glare
to his eyes gave spin. Alonzo bethought the moist
white woman. His sisters three warned him not to pair
with cotton femmes, but this one, la, his heart gave hoist.

He smiled. Another organ got gaved high hoist too.
"Victoria," he sent her name through his thin lips,
themselves the gift of some hot past bayou screw.
Be still! These paper piles stood tall, and oddity did slip

its foul way in. Toddlers, kids, teens, all stomach-pump sick.
So many! Were these just from since that nut
who claimed to be J Ed Hoover started his shtick?
May as well let him take over; Bureau making rut

by shedding directors left and right. Maybe I should
apply. First nig director of the FBI!
Take Mom and Grams from Louisiana swamp wood
to glitzy D.C. Shucks, ya'll, this nig's flyin' high!

You better back your coon ass up, tall Bro'.
Alonzo checked his figures. The Civic Center do: eight.
The Storyteller Fountain, Night One: ten showed.
And next day? Fifteen, some appearing late,

one and a half days. Montgomery stood a mess:
three dozen. He'd been nervous to let Vickie go
alone. But Dio and that Doberman, unless
he made mistake, could good care take. So he'd stayed no-go.

There'd been two more occasions: in Mobile
and Florence, with near the same results.
I ain't no CDC, but something bad fo' sho' do spill'.
And today, at ol' Vulcan, them two be spreadin' more mulch.

His voodoo shoulder—la, did it ever ache!
Jam his stomach with crawfish, Viennee weenies,
or grits—no matter. His shoulder gave him no break.
What it be sayin'? Someone, somewhere doing the meanies.

He mashed Vickie's number. How could she've been so dim
about that cell phone? /
                              "Alonzo? That you, dear heart?" /
At last she knew caller i.d. "Be me, your lover slim.
Mind if I go with to Vulcan? Something odd on my charts

"I gotta talk about." /
                              "My, let's do more than talk." /
Hot as usual. No one carry that from la femme.
He smiled to himself; but those figures still made balk.
Some bad, some where; he'd best ignore V's sexy glam.

The Bible say find something to save? No pearl, but the 'Ham.

Chapter Twenty-four: On the Mount with Vulcan's Iron Self

Alonzo, Vickie, Diogenes, the Furies, and a contingent of others drive up Red Mountain to oppose the Judge and J Edgar, who have plenty of supporters already present. Pluto shows up late, trailing Homeless Lena. Diogenes, once again, tries but fails to test the honesty of Alonzo Rankin, detective and lover. With both political factions, righteous fervor sends proof that plus and minus do not always cancel into zero.

Six kids stood pointing at Vulcan's bare ass,
which brought on snickers and giggles galore.
J Ed stood showing his usual class,
pontificating how commies keep America's store.

"You sleep; they stalk, masters of deceit!" /
Nearby, the Judge caressed a display of guns,
Touting Amendment Number Two. "We got to keep
'em, or bad government will make a counter-run.

"Don't snooze. Respect what Ed Hoover proves. They lie deep
in there, those commies and humanists, like apple-pie worms.
Look up! See that arrow ol' Vulcan keeps?
It's cast so sharp to give homos and commies squirms!"

A cheer began, and rows of boots began to stomp.
Three frightened ravens flew off. From their view on high,
they figured snakes or weasels gathered to feed and romp.
If only birds could sigh—but why do that, when you can fly?

Hot Dog Rita smiled and plied her ware with Cokes.
"Good U. S. A. dogs!" she cried. "No commies within!" /
"What are commies?" A young woman croaked.
An undergrad, she stayed limited in sin;

no such idea crossed her brain. Rita herself gave blink.
Had not her granddad fretted about them
shoving unions in, to make steel-workers slink?
"Something bad, I think. —My, aren't you pretty and slim!"

The college girl gave blush, took Rita's warm dog,
and smiled in thankful delight. /

                              "She's right;
you are," her boyfriend said. His little log
give stir. /

                "They're out there, bringing on a blight!"

J Ed and the Judge enjoined to shout.
"While you sleep, they're baking, but it's not bread!"
'Twas the Judge who gave this gastronomic fact rout.
"It's a virus, starting with letting unnaturals wed."

A slow chant began, "Let America Hate again!"
At this time, Vickie, Dio, and Alonzo showed.
"Where's red dog?" Lonz asked, as Furies out of his car gave spin.
"Need a van soon, 'way they multipled and growed."

Vickie nodded, happy at the fact. Seven now,
with two more coming today, from news Abby told.
But Alonzo was right. Pluto had left somehow.
"Where is he? Surely he didn't desert our fold,"

she asked of Dio, who shrugged.
                                            "Following the shill,"
came his reply. Before he could clarify,
tail-tucked, Pluto showed, displaying a will
to dog Homeless Lena, who was wandering wide

among the crowd, patting kiddies on their heads.
With each pat she gave a wiener, pointing them to
Hot Dog Rita's stand. A pied-piper shill, she led
their parents into buying, anointing them to

America's goodest dog. Sauerkraut or chili,
all was Chicago. And like the FBI guy gave said,
to eat any other way would be plain silly.
As Lena patted one more tot on its head,

Pluto snatched her oblong hot and ran oblique.
He spotted Lonz and dropped the foulness at his feet.
Dio saw his chance and sneaked his lantern—but it gave creak
and Lonz gave note. Unshorn, he jumped, escape complete.

Forlorn and frustrated, Dio stamped both feet.
Love-worn, Vickie grinned; she'd brush up on French,
'cause Creole Lonz was bright, handsome, and fleet.
Be-sworn, Pluto howled; his master had tossed a wrench:

Inspector Doberman, foiled by a Cynic.
But the woman would drop more of those tainted dogs,
of that Pluto kept certain. Muttness he'd have to mimic,
to keep tabs on Lena, so her memory he'd not jog.

The dropped dog hot? It got snatched by a cat.
Homeless Lena saw and let out a scream.
"That's not for you! Too much sodium, too much fat!"
The feline skittered off, quick and lean.

Dio felt empathy and offered Lena bucks
from his wallet crimson. "Thanks." She gave a snatch
while saying, "I don't really give two plucks
for cash. It's just that, durp, God's perfect creature is a cat.

"They should, durp, be eating fresh salmon and tuna—
at least raw liver and beefsteak, highest grade.
Lousy humans mistreat 'em. Humans to Luna,
I say—durp, thanks for the dough!—give cats rule and sway."

Dio's lantern sputtered—so hard he feared it out of gas.
But no, the meter regained its honesty flame.
To test, he shook it at a nearby boy and lass,
the sweet thing whose college knowledge had proved so lame.

A sputter and spiff. "What else is new in sports world,"
Dio bitterly asked. /
                            "Well, football season
is coming up." The college lass gave a twirl
with her finger. "Tickets is the only reason

"we stay in wretched school." She blew her boyfriend
a kiss. He might have fainted hadn't the Judge
whooped out a whoop so loud that it did send
the anxious crowd into a Sousa march to trudge

around the base of Vulcan. If Christians used prayer
wheels, many maledictions up could have been sent:
Dear Lord, fry commies, homos, malcontents in greasy air;
drown bookworms in paper slush; wall out immigrants.

What would baby Jesus do? He'd stomp 'em,
slash 'em, whip 'em, then crucify 'em all.
Says so in the Bible: *Thus the Lord did chomp 'em.*
A righteous coo sent hot gargle from all.

Their marching's synchronic thump did threaten to topple
Vulcan. But then a counter-clockwise trope did start!
In math it's said that minus will lay a whop full
on positive, leave it zero, snatch it like a shark.

Ye mathematicians dainty and proud, give heed!
The world alas, is with us far too much,
and whilst your number games make pretty screed,
this planet earth doth orbit with a crumbling crutch.

Just thus, the Furies and their humanist cohort
made counter-clockwise screech. "Don't let these dolts
push our intelligent values athwart.
Send them cooking pizzas, let beer keep them afloat!"

On what dire and angry gods did *these* folk give call?
Some hollered for Buddha, who'd plop a belly thick.
Some hollered for Darwin, who replaced monkeys for the Fall.
Some hollered for Bill Gates, whose Windows would slick

their very thoughts and fill their minds with sloth.
Some hollered for Hillary. Alas where had she gone?
Some for Bernie, some for Lady Gaga, so wroth
their thoughts. And just so, a righteous coo filled their throng.

Police arrived, or else plus and minus might
have burbled out warts no chemo ever could damp.
As it was, the stomping noise, it made awful blight,
to shiver trees, make children and squirrels decamp

to join those ravens three in stall formation above.
Anywhere but this where, many did think.
And they were right, for hate had shoved out love.
It left a wrathful, all-too-human stink.

Even Hot Dog Rita took leave, and certain parents
gathered little innocents, to keep them that way.
Others pushed theirs forth to say: "You daren't
not let our righteous thought have its sway."

Lena did stay. She cornered the hungry tomcat,
who busily gave bat at the hot dog Pluto had dropped,
its nose wriggling sniffs, its tongue hissing spats.
"Smart boy," Lena said. "You should never have copped

"that bad dog. Here, eat this can of sardines."
Lena peeled a tin and placed it on the ground,
snatching her sickly hot d. "You cats are kings and queens.
Humans? Well, durp, their kind should be put straight down."

She pocketed the tainted dog, where it would not be found.

Chapter Twenty-five: Weeks Pass, Clues Amass

Three weeks after the mathematical refutation at Vulcan, Alonzo surrounds himself with voodoo charms to study hard facts. (Pluto has tied three times to drop a tainted hot dog at Alonzo's feet. Each time, Diogenes and his lantern have interfered.) Alonzo's mystic shoulder attains a conclusion, which a surprise visit from Pluto, who brings a tainted hot dog that Homeless Lena dropped, confirms. Alonzo plans to take the hot dog to the police lab and calls Doc Eddie to further discuss his suspicions of Lena. Diogenes has followed Pluto, and he bursts in to try once more to give Alonzo the lantern test, but is thwarted by a most unnatural means.

A Santa Maria practitioner could not
have concentrated more. Alonzo leaned, he peered,
lit candles to the Virgin, gave Joseph a shot
of sacrificial rum. Still, he feared

for children of the 'Ham. Something amiss—
But what? And how? He mused: three times, Pluto had skipped
for him. Three times, ol' Dio's lantern had sent him remiss.
And now he watched candles in his apartment flick.

All these kids getting sick, while adults amassed
in throngs, spreading hatred thick, like Hellman's mayo.
Each group be glad to get the other gassed.
But kids, they mattered most! Did they not show the way o'

our future, bright or crass? What if no kids left in the 'Ham?
Not just the 'Ham, but all this wrecked-up state!
Alonzo studied his stats. They etched some plan,
of that he stayed certain. Would his decipher come too late?

Montgomery, Mobile, Florence, some burg mid-state
by name of Livingston. Live not for long, at least its kids.
Hot Dog Rita had been at each do, selling plates
of "no-commie dogs." Health inspection put hard skids

on blaming her. Hell, he had gobbled dozens.
And even Vickie's lips partook a few.
So if not Rita . . . what 'bout her bag lady cousin,
Homeless Lena? Sure! She dropped dogs from the blue,

patting lice-thick toddler heads, dispensing grins
like she some misplaced swampy voodoo queen.
Was *she* who send good tots and teens into dark zombie spins?
But why? Her motive—nutty as envy's green?

Alonzo's shoulder gave twitch, which he could not ignore.
Do something, cher! (Yes, his shoulder could talk!
And in bilingual, fractured Frenglish, what's the more!)
That Pluto chien be giving Lena the stalk.

Lonz loved his shoulder, a gift from his gram,
who knew swamp potions, cures, and hexes too.
Her shoulder spoke to her this same, sent warn of wicked plans.
Homeless Lena, his shoulder said, *she bad voodoo.*

Alonzo tapped his iPhone. He'd give Doc Eddie
a call. The guy, he'd treated Lena. He and Doc were skin,
a different tint, but close enough and steady.
The Doc would know what Homeless held within.

He'd shout bad news out, if asked, about Lena.
A lowly street-head for sure, but something deeper?
Socio? Some eight-dollar Doc-word to mean a
serial-killer mission, proclaim Lena a sleeper?

Alonzo phoned, got la ol' answering machine.
He left a message for a meeting tomorrow.
Then came strange scratching at his door. His spleen
remembered Poe's "Raven." *But I got no sorrow,*

no lost Lenore. I do have me Vickie, by the good Lord.
He rushed for the rapping; 'twas not his heart's desire,
but Pluto, clamping a hot dog aboard,
in slobber jaws. Lonz bent, got of sudden inspired.

"Merci, chien." He took the dog and gave a sniff.
"To the lab this will go. Come on in. Viennee
Weenies be all I got." Pluto gave a whiff.
"Don't let them candles scare. Pad in, stay a teeny."

Pluto sauntered and sat before the Blessed Virgin.
"Good 'cision," Lonz said. "That Lady protect us all.
I'll fetch them weenies. Two cans, I be splurgin'
'cause a this." He held up the hot dog. "I'ma call

"it to lab, mon cher." /
                              Just then Dio rushed the door,
having followed Pluto. With lantern held high,
he screamed, "Fair judgment this time, of that I'm sure."
Pluto's rear end gave happy wag, the BVM did fly,

knocking *le lampe sacré* from Dio's hand
onto Alonzo's hardwood floor. And there it broke.
The Blessed Virgin's pale face looked up, bland.
"See, told you. Virgin Mary never blow no smoke."

The BVM, she smiled so sweet and with such class,
was like the Mona Lisa and Whistler's momma
all popped in one. Dio, though, he huffed a blast.
Was a mother who started his earthly trauma,

and now a mother had ended his holy quest.
He stared at lantern pieces splayed about his feet.
He beat his thighs, his head. "No rest, no rest!" /
"*Cher*, be calm. Fresh out of crawfish, but Vienee's compete."

Alonzo set BVM upright, gave Pluto a pat,
then turned to tsk at the mumbling god-dad
of Vickie, not wanting to cause a spat
of blood bad twixt the old guy, who looked jailhouse sad.

In floor-grief, Dio squirmed and let these words drop:
"Lord Hades, you've done done your sourest trick yet!"
He rolled, he tugged his zipper thing, hoping to flop
his penis in protest. Nada. Only his drool got wet. /

"Stand up, *mon cher*. Be mannish. Get you a new one.
I'ma drive you to the sporting store,
buy a orange vest for Pluto, bullets for my gun,
and two lanterns for each your hand, maybe more.

"But now, let's eat Viennee weenies. Got 'nuff cans I'm sure."

Chapter Twenty-six: Victoria Frets, Stumbles, and Marvels

Victoria is walking the streets before the public library. She's returned there many times, even Googled herself. But those articles brought on only angst, not nostalgia or enlightenment. Too much was repeating. Instead of righteous Comstock, there was the Hoover creep; instead of hypocritical Preacher Beecher, there was Judge Roy Bean Too. Do eternal Hindu spirals present the fate of the human race? She thinks of her Furies. Anger, anger, anger. That and pride pervade their ranks, despite her admonitions to Abby. She'd read of Stephen Hawking's death and his theory of the AI singularity. In her previous life, she'd thought of Darwin as a savior of sorts, foretelling the evolution of free love and the demise of hate, the fruit of eugenics. But now, she worries, does an entirely different evolution lie in wait? Just where did eugenics lead Hitler and his crew? Surely no! A newspaper can change not just opinion, it can elucidate facts. She marvels. A newspaper! Why hasn't she already thought of that?

That Victoria was not prone to cry
did not preclude a good long pout.
Which led to a heated walk, which sent her by
the downtown library, which nearly gave her rout,

thinking of the Comstock/Hoover equation,
the Judge Bean/Beecher preacher similitude,
—enough sadness to hop a beam-me-down station.
On top, her spirit guide had turned quite rude,

with swinging his lantern, barking like his dog,
forever rubbing his log. And where did he sleep?
She'd rented a house near Alonzo, her prime love grog,
whose mocha light had thrust her free love stance down deep

onto some derelict back street. She lit a cig.
Could not have done so way back when, on taking walks.
Might as well have worn a scarlet A and done a jig.
Bankers would faint, society bluebloods would balk.

She exhaled a stream and blinked when a lad,
Teutonic blonde, scratched a hip as he strolled by.
She inhaled, she exhaled, her stream lightsome and glad.
From instinct, she almost winked a flirty eye.

Instead, she swayed and dropped the cig. Really, she was glad
to solo tangle with Lonz. Life was running high.
She found even his voodoo to be—quite rad,
in lingo of this time—kin to spirit mimes gone by.

No, even street heat could not cause sighs! She got loads
of cash from the gods in Hades, surplus to feed
her Furies . . . still, Dio stayed a worry. His goads
came daily. No matter how she might plead,

he left each night with Pluto. If not a wine jug,
then some appliance box his nightly bed,
of that she stayed certain. She'd watched one being lugged
two blocks back, into a makeshift, homely tin shed.

Two men, its claimants, had panhandled her.
She'd given each a Lincoln—her favorite President,
of course. Had he lived, he'd not have be-scandaled her,
not allowed her and Tennie to become resident

in those filthy Tombs. Which thought returned her to Dio.
Hardcore hermit, he'd never lug a mattress to a shed.
"Carrion Comfort!" Was that a quote? Some poet guy-o?
Yes, Hopkins. He and Dio. Their obsessive dread

of "thingdom's thrum," as Dio gave its said, kept rule.
V spied Homeless Lena squatting on a library bench.
The newest Fury named Slam Sam thought Lena cool;
Abby and the others, they thought her a wench.

Alonzo suspected her in high detective fashion.
Of what, V was unsure, though he'd set a meeting
with Doc today, he of the endless rations
in his cornucopia car. In a heat wave fleeting

she envisioned the Doc pulling a wine jug
from the trunk of that amazing car. Such would not
surprise . . . nor would Lena's role as some infectious bug.
. . . That local plague when I lived in England . . . they thought

it caused by a Pied Piper's infected candy.
He came before the kindergarten I started,
praise Athena. V smiled: my one concept that worked dandy.
How many others, alas, had departed,

all but stillborn, like my poor son. Was life just a spiral?
Just heat swirling streets with random bumps?
Back in Hades, the Buddha had gone viral
as he sat by the Styx in ponder. Rumors were he thumped

head, feet, and fists into its bank, when downward first he came.
Enraged for three centuries, unbelieving himself thrown
once more into life and not Nirvana. All the same,
there he'd sat, like other poor mortals, seed sown

again, again.
                    V watched Lena pet a tabby,
put down a can of sardines. A mother and child walked by,
and Lena stuffed a hot dog in the kid's shabby
paw, which he sniffed and ate, while Momma gave the eye

to some cop. Oh my, it was Smith. Well maybe a lady
in his life would send him calm good—or get *her* beat.
Spirals, spirals. V mused. Life flows dank and shady.
Was there no reprieve, no spot to offer something sweet?

More mothers with strollers strolled by,
more teens ogled each other in their double heat,
more dogs, more cats—life was teeming its thighs!
But teeming with what? Hatred and spite, or love so fleet?

On a post she leaned. In England, Darwin had ruled supreme.
Education, they'd thought. Eugenics, good breeding.
Not long after her own death, Hitler'd shown his spleen,
exposing to all just where those plans were leading.

The kid grabbed his tummy. Lena trotted away,
followed by the tabby. Inter-species love
remained more common than human interplay.
The kid started to bawl; his sister gave a shove.

He fell to the ground, emitting pink bile.
His sister screamed, "I didn't do it!"
The mother slapped her, then forced a smile,
on seeing Vickie watch. "Don't know how I get through it!"

she shouted. A prime example, V decided,
for planning parenthood and just saying no.
That wheelchair guy though—good no one unglided
his birth. All those missing strings and black holes,

not to mention the Singularity that Hawking foretold.
Ah yes, V thought as the woman shook first her son,
then her daughter. Let computers unfold;
we humans have surely ended our wretched run.

She then remembered Alonzo, her sister Tennie C,
her daughter—even her husbands three weren't always bad.
Put dismal Lord Hades behind thee! Keep free.
This green and blue globe's whirls aren't always sad.

Look at Dio, swinging that lantern for two thousand years,
as if he were mad. A bastion of optimism!
One interview with him would waylay everyone's fears.
—Of course! That's how she'd been loosed from prison!

The daily papers exposed all lies. Revive *Woodhull*
and Claflin, her and Tennie C's grand old rag.
V looked: the woman was giving her son the full
hug treatment. Her daughter joined in. Anger had flagged.

Newspapers! V danced a jig. *An old trick from my young bag.*

Chapter Twenty-seven: Gallop Shows

Just when Victoria has the newspaper epiphany that promises to ease her blue funk, a strange dancing and singing creature makes theatrical appearance before Birmingham Public Library.

V danced her happy jig. Newspapers! They would show
the righteous way, would turn misinformation
into a truthful, pure, and guiding glow.
Printer's ink! Since Gutenberg, it's lent dissemination!

As if evoked, an old black man joined her dance.
No, he was white, and he was tapping his feet.
Wait. Might it be a woman, some kin perchance
to Lena? Whichever, a smile so greased and neat

emitted that V felt freed from every sin.
A passing car pulled curbside, then another.
The library's windows showed faces peeping from within.
The dancer clapped long musical hands and shouted, "Brother!

"Sister! Cousin! Nephew and niece! Gather round me
and listen. I got the goods, believe me!
I know the score! Just follow my bleats and tweets
They'll heave truth your way, they won't deceive thee!

"The Web's the Way, ye ol' Information Highway!
It sings without effort, so fast, so speedy.
No need to ponder, it'll promote thy way,
it'll buttress thine vision, make it less seedy.

"Your flower will blossom, then regurgitate!
Yes, like a momma dog feeding her nine puppies!
Shout out! Lift up! You can even levitate!
Yes! Yes! The Net has turned us all so lucky!" /

The woman, her kids, Smith, all stopped to watch
as the person, whatever its sex, stood to spin
a ballroom dance. Then came a lovely shock,
for its mouth sang song derived from some wondrous glen:

> "Give me a dime, I'll give you Truth.
> Make it a quarter, I'll wrap it in youth.
> Give me a buck, it'll take on shine.
> Give me ten, it'll taste like wine.

Hell, give me a penny, I'm not proud,
your new Truth will dismay any crowd.
Just give, give, give, and whatever you care to hear
will glow from building tops, clarion and clear.
Give, give, give. I'll polish, I'll rhyme
whatso you want, lending its mush a spine.
"Give, give, give. 'Hey, what is Truth?' asked ol' Pilate,
ahead of his time. Did that sweet guy let
some fact send flop? He sure as heck didn't.
Give, give, give. Don't keep your good Truth hidden!
Truth's a fine mirage, it's a polished mirror
to show your very best you in. Truth's a grand seer or
a loving prophet, into whose box you can fit
neat as microchips aligning binary bits.
Truth! I store more than fifty shades that'll win you!
Truth! And every shade will surely send you
your soul's deep need. Truth, Gluth, Bluth, Sputh!
Whatev'. I'll polish it all with a lustrous youth!
Hey! You shouldn't believe all that you hear!
That much I'll grant as being quite clear.
Just choose sources wisely to reflect your best you;
don't fret about walking in no one else's shoes.
In other words, stay careful just where you steer!
Pre-sort! Uncertainty you'll never fear.
Truth? It's what you know for sure and hold quite dear.
That's the best Truth! That will render you into sheer
granite wonder—or mayhap more pliable.
(For you really don't want to be held liable.)
Give, give, give. My Truth's reliable.
And just who am I? It's undeniable:
Gallop is my name, and Truth is my game.
That's with an 'o,' not with no durned lame
'u' Why? Because with Web Truth I do run
to spread things spidery, under rays of sun.
Silken and clean, O how it will cling!
Brazen and bold, O how it will ring!
Your Truth, that is . . . all others I'll fling!

The man or woman gave a courteous bow.
The whole library'd emptied to watch its fine show.
All clapped, agreeing that this creature knew how
to make truth spin just like a wondrous top and go

first left, then right, then up, but never down.
They tossed jewels, quarters, bills, and they clapped
as its dance got did. Waltz? Two-step? Such a fine clown,
no thought to form did they give. Bread and circus zapped.

They shillied, they shallied, they laughed, they cried.
They hugged, they patted, they kissed each other.
"Bluth truth!" they shouted. "Anything else is a lie!"
From its cloak, the creature tossed a blanket to smother

their shouts first into cooing, then hot angry garble.
Each dancer forsook the other, like dervishes
a-twirl in grand solipsistic marvel.
"*My* Truth! *My* Bluth!" bumped soon into skirmishes.

Fisticuffs and shouts, some kicks, some screams.
As fingers pointed and elbows flailed,
outlanders intruding on insular dreams.
That lively jig, alas, too soon gave way to wails.

High up above: a TV dish. Atop it, three black birds.
One flew up, then a second, then the other.
So high did they aspire, no need of lying words.
In great Zen non-truth's truth did they hover.

Far down below, V felt drained. She feared a relapse.
Oh kind Mr. Hawking, could you indeed be right?
Your Singularity, could it offer last hope perhaps?
Are we humans nothing but earth's pimply blight?

Of sudden, as she walked home, day dropped into night.

Chapter Twenty-eight: Diogenes Shops for Sporting Goods

Diogenes gets driven to a sporting goods store, where Alonzo fulfills his promise to buy him two lanterns and Pluto a vest. Unsurprisingly, neither lantern is able to measure honesty. Dio, Pluto, and Alonzo squabble over fashion design.

His word stayed gold. Alonzo soon was driving
both Dio and Pluto to Sporting Goods Galore.
There, the three stared hard at a wall of thriving
assault rifles, assured by a clerk that whole lots more

slept stored in back. "We're ready for the Singularity,"
the clerk offered. /
                           "Ah la. Just what be that?" /
"When college brains and computers rise up to seize
home rule. Thick books, thin veggies. No smoked bacon fat.

"This here will take good care of them, and that." The clerk
gave lean to lend an AR-15 his sloppy smooch. /
"Just three boxes of bullets, cher. Need them for work,
police discount, please." /
                           When the white kid doubted that truth,

Alonzo showed his shiny badge. They then bought
two lanterns; Dio insisting he needed flame,
no battery glow. Right there, before he got caught
he lit one in the store, displaying no shame,

desiring most to test-run the Mocha Fellow.
The flame burned steady, Dio's eyes grew wide.
He then strolled toward the clerk, who turned un-mellow:
"You can't light that in here. Flames we don't abide

"with all this gunpowder and ammo lying about." /
"The stuff you're saving for the Singularity?" /
The clerk's face twisted. "That's right. Put it out."
The lantern burned. Just so. It tested no rarity

in human nature, no one honest man nor gal.
"Your light's too light," Dio addressed the Coleman.
He trimmed the wick, knowing he'd have to visit hell
and consult with Vulcan, if ever he'd get to show man

exhibiting at least one honest case.
Meanwhile, Pluto chomped down on a hunter pink vest.
"You have no taste." Dio tugged the vest back to its place.
Pluto tugged it back again. They would have had no rest

if Lonz hadn't snatched, then tossed it in his cart.
"Let Pooch decide. And let's take some gift to Vickie,
I'ma celebrate today." /
                              Dio then showed greasy art
by tossing smarm and flattery spiffy:

"A man of your honesty should celebrate *every* day.
If people knew, they'd bestow the keys to B'ham City." /
Alonzo's left eye twitched, to balance his shoulder's sway.
"What you be do, old man?" /
                              Dio thought, *I'm sitting pretty.*

No flattery moves him. The end to my quest.
A truly honest man here stands before me.
I'll pop down to Hades, bring back Vulcan's best,
Eureka! Old Hades and Zeus can't then ignore me. /

"You ask why today? You was there! Pooch jaw a tricky clue.
That my celebrate! Pluto go snoop on my task.
Inspector Hound! He be a true bright gumshoe.
—Hey, leave that pink vest be. Pooch get to bask

"in what color he want. He tote me the proof,
I'ma take it to lab, talk the what with Doc,
then go 'rest Lena, who more than some homeless goof—
say, cher, look at them violet sandal. They rock.

I'ma still see V' pretty toes." /
                              "She matched Hoover's
toenail polish. 'Least that's what she said." /
"If he gon' play in Alabam' he best buy remover.
Him and that Judge, they sure sleep in one odd bed."

Just like you and V, D thought. *One alive, one dead.*
He held up a lantern and made to point.
When Pluto and Lonz gave look, D tossed the pink dread
vest under cowboy boots. /
                              "I'ma disappoint,"

Lonz said, as Pluto gave snort to reclaim the hot pink vest.
"You old, but still cannot always get you way." /
D bowed his head. Eternity loomed without rest.
Bad enough false-hoping his lantern would sway

on some honest bloke. Now Pluto in pink array?

Chapter Twenty-nine: Diogenes Visits Hades' Repair Shop

Diogenes further tests the two Coleman lanterns. As he suspects, they only give a steady glow and don't measure honesty at all. Before descending to Hades to get his old lantern repaired, he makes a brief visit to Victoria's house, where an especially man-hating Fury gives him chase. Slipping on down to Hades, he trudges his way to Vulcan's repair shop, only to find that Vulcan has passed out from too much wine. But an apprentice takes over and repairs the sacred lantern of discernment. Lord Hades sends Dio back to the world, giving his usual double-edged encouragement.

Diogenes, forever a sport, did give both Coleman
lanterns eight other tries. A steady burning flame
revealed eight "honest" folk. *Not tricking this old man.*
Defective. What a shame. Yet all the same

he eyed once more yon napping mellow cop,
as Pluto pranced by, in his hot pink vest.
"It'd be a compliment to say you look a fop,"
D muttered. With a whine, Pluto lay down to rest

beside the napping cop. Dio tip-toed.
A flame steady yes, but a no-go test. He made ready
to head to Hades, stopping off the road
by Vickie's place.
                    There, she looked depressed, unsteady.

"Go visit your nice napping mocha man,"
Dio suggested. /
                    "Men!" one of the Furies hissed.
Dio, being one, took his leave in the span
of one Mississippi. /
                    "You won't be missed!"

that Fury shouted. Slam Sam was this one's name,
if he recalled correct. She seemed vying to oust
Abby, maybe even Vickie herself, if it came
to that. Dio gave himself a roust,

smoothed down his pants and that damnable zipper,
gathered his lamp's pieces, told V that he'd be at
the repair shop, in Vulcan's domain. (A nipper
of wine, he'd swing hot tongs, char folk on the back

unless aware they kept.)
> A likely ATM machine

proved indeed to be a cranky Beam-Me-down.
No room for Pluto. Just as well, for in that hot pink scream
he resembled a feline in a wedding gown.

What sport in Hades they would make of them!
Plenty 'nough jokes already got cast by big wigs
about a guard dog and some foolish Greek whose thin
hopes for one honest mortal snapped daily like twigs.

Dio crawled in; the machine whirred its torture
to land him in east Hades.
> *Where's that blessed shop?*
Drop off the big road by the waxed apple orchard . . .
take one left . . . then another . . . then stop . . .

Wait! Count six snakes that slither by . . . (no doubt the warped
Rorschach intent of some Lord Hadeian prank),
Wade through the lemon Jell-O stream that always morphed
that no-step-in-twice adage into cloying yellow yank.

That's right, Heraclitus! Just watch me step not twice
but thrice in this mess we call a world.
Stick to fishing, pal, forget deep thought, my advice.
It only makes your Greek neurons unfurl.

Just listen to me! I sound like Doc Eddie.
Next I'll rent his FMRI machine,
beam it down under here, try to steady
on Lord Hades. As Dio tugged from the Jell-O stream,

he glanced back to see Mother Teresa offering hot tea
to the Buddha, suffering his perennial fit
at ixnayed Nirvana, at being kept in life's tossed sea.
Beside them, Saint Francis and a squirrel did chit.

Dio trudged. He crossed a street paved in mold, and . . . Eureka!
There the tin-covered shop sat, under a dead live oak. /
"You're here sooner than I thought. Come down to seek a
repair? Got that busted lantern there in your poke?

"How'd it happen, pal?" /
> Hades wore a leather apron,

no doubt protecting that forked dong of his.

Like all men, he held his precious as saffron.
Must be nice, though, to pluck it without a tiz.

Diogenes thought this, then asked, "Where's Vulcan?" /
"Thor," Lord Hades corrected. /
                                    Good, a Norse day.
Hades kept more chipper on them, less sulking.
D explained about the BVM and her sway

that knocked his lantern to the floor, where the impact
left it— /
           "That woman and her son always stir the show.
Packed both back Mid East ways, where stirs stay fact.
Did keep the old man here, as apprentice, you know." /

With a nod, Dio opened his rucksack and spilled
its within. On the table twenty pieces rattled.
"Um, I was hoping . . . Thor—" /
                                  "He's chilled."
Lord Hades made a tippling motion and cackled.

"Eight bottles of an aging stout red. He'll be out
for three days, to rise like—well you know *that* old tale.
But don't you fret, someone near as good, no lout,
is handling his shop and forge, without fail.

"Sweet ol' Joseph—the BVM's hubbie dear,
though just what *that* ever got him—" Hades popped his middle—
"Well, the sexual antics of mortals create one shear
mystery to me. Want to leave it here? Joe's apt to fiddle

"with it a fortnight or more. Carpenter by trade,
metal gives him fatigue." Hades smiled at his pun,
which D grudgingly wished that he had made. /
"No, in a rush and all, trouble's being spun—

"say, you don't suppose those two sneaked over
from the Mid-East, do you?" /
                              Hades gave his balls
an itch, which turned Dio envious green as clover
(which grew red in Hades). "How's Joe at fixing overhauls?

"These seem to be stuck." /

"To answer query one:
The BVM's nervous about flying in jets,
so I doubt they made that trip. And you know the son
stays tangled in Mommy's apron strings. All bets

"are off for him to stray away. As far as query two,
you're up top in the modern, with-it age,
so don't you think their clothing styles should do?" /
At that, Joseph walked in, hunched, almost a sage

in appearance. When he saw the lantern he balked.
"You don't want that metal stuff. It rusts, gets
fatigued." /

Dio inhaled and shut his eyes. Had he walked
hard into jokes from a minstrel show? /

"Your best bet,

"seems to me, is one of cedar—no I retract,
its oil is flammable. Got some nice heavy oak.
Let me start up now, measure your hand for exact
tension and grip, so it won't slip and croak

like this metal stuff tends to do." /

Hades gave a
smile, then slapped the hunched guy's back. Joseph howled.
"Whoops, forgot." Hades turned to Dio. "Thor's tongs made a
hot blister there, just before Thor turned wine-foul.

"But don't you fret. Old Joe here's up to the job.
"He'll have it in a jiff. Pshaw. Next time, save a
min for a social call. Some gods and I were giving lob
to a minotaur's head and Zeus asked, just as I made a

goal, if your lantern shtick still goes, if it's
still on sterile track. —Oh look, ol' Joe's done done.
Told you he was speedy. Just look, it's a spiff.
Hope the *wood* don't catch fire, that *wouldn't* be no fun.

D stomped his foot. Hades was stealing all the puns.
"Gotta go," he mumbled. /

"Sure, sure. Don't never stop.
We'll roast a gold goose, if'n you find just one honest one." /
Ol' Joe showed a Skilsaw. "Wish I'd had this back in my shop.

"Could've churned out crosses like water drops."

Chapter Thirty: Alonzo and Doc Eddie Share Action

Pluto carries two poisoned hot dogs to Alonzo, who's confirmed his shoulder twitch suspicion about Homeless Lena. He consults with Doc Eddie, who's surprised since he's had Lena in a long study, undergoing FMRIs.

With Pluto wearing the hot pink vest as disguise,
Homeless Lena had tossed him two more wieners,
then added, "Take one to your wretched master, whose eyes
must crystal cross in a axonic's sheen or

some other bling a kitty—durp—would know to avoid."
Now Lonz showed those two dogs in a plastic evidence bag
and Doc Eddie replied, "Believe me, I'm annoyed
I didn't catch this. My FMRI's must lag

in some unforeseen way, though just of late
they proved a fact most amazing." Doc Eddie bit
his lip. He'd promised to not let out that V was a shade,
especially to this detective fellow, for those two lit

on one another in some supernal way
that outshone earth's—or hell's!—metaphysics.
"Give 'em time," Dio'd advised. "Truth will out, but till that day
let joy have sway. Don't fret. Sad Truth always sticks its

sharp-forked tongue out." /
                                    Now Doc inspected the bag.
"A psychopath. Before today I'd judged her rants
about kit-cats the standard American jag.
A wag once claimed that if French poodles were advanced

"to fight in Vietnam we'd retreat that selfsame day.
And if Sandy Hook had been a fancy pet spa
assault rifles would have right then scooted on their lame way." /
"So you be say Lena make some kit-cat hurrah?" /

"Indeed. She always claims humans belong on Luna,
leave this globe to cats." /
                                    "Make Earth a litter box?
And leave behind one big ration of tuna?" /
" 'We humans,' " Doc Eddie sighed, " 'make a foul pox.' "

The Doc was quoting Diogenes, caught in
a moment of black. "Don't do what I preach,"
D had then shrugged, swaying the lantern he'd bought in.
"Hits me now and then, when honest seems out of reach."

Now Doc Eddie told Lonz, "Let's take my car.
She's used to getting toted therein. Convince her
she's riding to a galaxy long ago and far
away. Some paid FMRI's. Might fly, since her

main cash stash has come from doing the same
with me." /
         And so they rode away to find Lena.
Lonz said, "Can we stop ahead? I got a flame
for some café au lait." /
                "This car's my mom's, means a

"lot to me. Push that far blue button on your right."
They passed a Wendy's; still, Lonz did as he was told.
A red espresso machine slid out, a mystic delight.
"How you like it," Doc asked. "Light, medium, or bold?"

Before night had come, Lena, durp, sat in the hold.

Chapter Thirty-one: Victoria Consults with the Furies

Victoria wants to revive her old newspaper, Woodhull and Claflin's Weekly. *Abby and the four original Furies convince her to go Internet instead, while Slam Sam hatches other plans, and while Gallop, spying outside, hatches the grandest plan of all by sending twelve remaining Furies deep into their iPhones.*

Though the young faces before her glowed, V did fret,
for a hue unnatural soaked them, a bluish tint
she'd not seen yet. Was like an incubus had spat
hot sperm. From hell or heaven was it sent?

"My greater-great aunt," she gave start and lied,
"ran a newspaper in New York City.
Free love and education were the truths she plied,
exposing bad politicians without pity."

Her Furies sat listening intently on the floor—
at least those who were not tapping their iPhones,
that is. Abby jerked up: "Newspapers are a bore.
What we need, Ms. V, to pull people in the zone

"are Twitter, glitter blogs on the Internet."
V twitched. Alonzo had warned about this blend:
"Kids win two rounds of some game and think they've been shat
out of the Blessed Virgin Mother's rear end."

She thought, *Live and learn. Or better, resurrect.*
Of 18 Furies, 12 sent supernal glow
from the pads in their hands. She checked
herself from putting on a raging show.

In Queen V's London, there'd been gin mills;
in Tweed's New York, laudanum. The Bible got it right:
The poor are always with us. When not, these new ills
arise. Even the underworld had its blights

with Lord Hades shaking Styx like a carpet,
or slipping cockroaches in the ambrosia.
V chided herself: *Think positive, gal. You shouldn't let
life's thunderstorms take hold and hose ya*

onto some isolated, lonely, rocky shore.
"Abby!" Vickie beamed. "Okay, let's move with the times!
You and the others gear up! Show me how to pour
out trustworthy news, our fine truth that rhymes

with free love and peace. Darwinian education!"
Abby and the four sisters, with all good grace, beamed back.
"Computers are what we need to move this nation!"
While those five gave out cheers, Slam Sam, she planned a hack

more direct than any computer. She'd return
to the good ol' days when B'ham was known
as Dynamite City. But this time penises would burn,
not Blacks.   Through a window thin Gallop peeped, hard blown

by solipsism's whirling wind. Gallop espied
the dozen on their iPhones, then Slam Sam knotting
herself in a corner alone. What grandeur doth lie
with ignorance and hate! That pair render plotting

their sister chaos simple, like stacking alphabet blocks.
The five first Furies consulted on buying computers.
Slam Sam, insulted, bethought an uncle who blasted rocks
somewhere north of the Ham. A lech, he'd scoot her

way if she showed just one nipple. Gallop had sneaked
inside to magically weave the dozen iPhones.
"What?!" "How?!" "Why?!" From twelve Furies leaked
incredulous anger. They forgot V, to pout alone.

Thus did one group twist to fourteen, to make a combat zone.

Chapter Thirty-two: Another Charmer from Sweet Home Alabama

Wherein soon-not-to-be Attorney General Bereft Sessions receives a call from the Judge and J. Ed. Bereft puts them on hold to oversee some refugee and marijuana mitigation litigation.

"What? Oh Judge Bean, such a dear old friend. Put him on." /
The Honorable Bereft Sessions frowned at his phone.
Computer screens about did keep his eyes on glom—
images of brown-skinned creatures sneaking through zones

of good U. S. desert, clutching babes to their teats,
while gibbering garbled, outlandish tongues—
these held him thrall. /
                    "Bereft? Roy here. I have a truly neat
notion to reclaim our land, rid it of pothead bums." /

"Tell him my birthday was just last week," a voice insisted. /
"Roy? You're breaking up. Who was that? A little filly?" /
"It's J Ed. He fights commies, listed or unlisted.
Our plan is to hoist commandments that will really

"punch out false non-believers who still linger
in good Alabama towns. Think you can push a Granite
Grant? That's what we'll call it. Snappy, eh? A stinger!" /
A bank of screens near Bereft showed—drowning the planet—

marijuana smoke, pipes, roach clips, rolling papers.
They burst from city dumps, they dropped from tall buildings,
and grasping them all were kids bent out of shape or
suffering Severe Dope Malformation. Some geldings

appeared, some slut mothers with mixed race kids
still clinging to their arms and boobs . . . /
                    "Bereft? You there? /
"My hundredth anniversary with the Bureau can't skid
by unnoticed." /
            Bereft ran fingers through his hair.

Computers on his right showed brown-skinned creatures;
computers on his left showed dropping paraphernalia. /
"Bereft! These granite commandments could feature
in every Alabama town. Imagine how swell ya'll

"look. Maybe this can get ya back in graces with
that orange-hued guy." Since they were standing in a mall,
the judge noted a pert teen. Could he change places with
her mother? J. Ed, meanwhile, spied an antique stall.

"Tell him there's an Empire chest of drawers that would fit
in my bedroom. For my work anniversary, I mean." /
"Hush. —Bereft, I know you've a lot on your mind. I could flit
up—" /
        "We can wipe out commies!" /
                              "Kill mommies? That's obscene,

"Roy. Come to your senses." All the computer screens
began to roll, as if old time TVs. Hashish smoke
like tornadoes, milk-filled brown tits, kids screaming.
"Gotta go, Roy. The state we're in's no joke." /

"Commies everywhere. I've seen eighteen just last hour!" /
"The humanists are rampant! The Second Commandment—
Amendment, I mean. We need it to stay in power." /
"You creep! Police! I saw where your hand went!" /

"Roy, Roy. That I heard. Why don't you try college girls?
Gotta go, really. Goodbye to you and your odd friend." /
"Wait up, Bereft! This plan we have will unfurl
the troubles in our land. Honest! Look, I'll send

"the entire Alabama map, all its cities and towns,
courthouse squares from B'ham to Eppes. Bereft? You there?"
The Judge frowned. "He put me on hold!" Not one to stay down,
he eyed a blonde with a doll. Too young? He kept *some* flare. /

J Ed had pulled out index cards to follow a black guy
who looked a lot like that supposed cop. One Ubangi
squares like another, he thought. All commies, just sly
in how they slink. They'll leave America dangly

with those protests of theirs. That's how the commies start:
one little chip here, one brick cracked there.
Soon enough they're at the second amendment's heart.
Am I being unfair? He blinked. The Judge was giving stare

at some blonde girl and her doll. "Roy, Roy, we gotta go find
a sculptor. No time for that." /
                                    "A Christian one?" /
Yes, yes, Christian and smitten like Saul, blind." /
The Judge waved at the girl, who to her doll clung. /

"The phone book's what I suggest. Yellow Pages." /
"No, J Ed. We'll use computers and Google." /
Toward the library they scurried, where rages
were happening since three blogs were shaking noodles

enough to keep the head librarian from her doodles.

Chapter Thirty-three: The Library Prepares for a Second Workout

Another brawl is building at Birmingham's Public Library. The Judge and J Ed join in, searching for a Christian sculptor to chisel out the first of their many planned granite monuments celebrating the good old days and the Commandments Ten. They come in contact with a mother of a daughter studying sculpture at a nearby university. J Ed consults with the mother about her daughter. Diogenes shows at the library, where he's planned to meet with Doc Eddie. To the happy surprise of Diogenes, Alonzo accompanies the good doctor there. Diogenes is sure the caffeine he's just drunk will enable his test.

B'ham's library had just dried firehose water
from what its faithful workers called the Disney Scam.
But now it seemed another book slaughter
already lay in plan: three blogs were stirring flim-flam

about free love education. Most patrons kept Googling
poodles, thank Zeus, since the AKC's pet parade
gave glow. "How cute!" /
          "How sweet!" /
                  "Those eyes!" /
                            "That tail!" Most kept
      flügling,
enhancing barks and whimpers snooty owners made.

Some others, though, gave droop into a different chute,
to watch a woman running for President, tooting
for sex and drug education. "She's sorta cute,"
an older fellow offered. /
                "A wench! she'll have kids rooting.

"They'll be humping in halls and smoking that pot." /
Another podcast showed the Five First Furies swaying
in unit.
          Judge Roy walked in, gave that screen a shot,
which set his eyeballs, which set his lower balls, a-braying. /

"They'll leave their locker rooms! They'll all be humping!" /
"Commies," J Ed sent shout, "start out this same way."
Some patrons raised their brows. "They start out thumping
our textbooks, they end up bumping our American Way." /

"He's right," Judge Roy added. "We need to return
to the good ol' days." /

An aging black patron

gave twitch. She still ached with scars from the burns
inflicted by the 16th Street church bomb. A matron

at one time, now forgotten, she roamed the streets
to shouts of "Step along, witchy woman!"
She thought, *Even bumming Third Avenue sure beats*
those "good ol' days." She left to continue her roaming

at a where more safe than what was building here.
Roy and J Ed stayed. They roused indignant shouts.
"Nothing's wrong with our education. It's plain fear
that woman's selling, her and her commie louts!" /

"My friend is right. Instead of pumping weights
and running on God's grassy green sport fields,
kids'll be surfing their iPads for hookup dates;
instead of eating fried chicken and praying, they'll snort pills,

"they'll push around no-good unwedlocked babies,
they'll worship Satan, sacrifice kit-cats and puppy dogs!"
That last smoldered the AKC fans, like rabies.
Judge Roy stepped forth and coughed. "Humanist hogs

"will get their just desserts, if we can install—" /
"in every good commie-free Alabama town—" /
"a great granite statue of the perfumed burning bush wall—"
(Judge Roy had spied a pre-teen and let his guard down.) /

"My friend means those Commandments Ten. We're here
to search out a good Christian sculptor, whose talents—" /
"Like Jesus told the Pharisees, to make life clear:
Don't bury your talent. Armor it with valence!" /

"Excuse me sirs, but my little boy uses modeling clay
and goes to church three times in each and every week." /
"Ma'am, we need something durable—" /

"Though he knoweth the Way

he must yet showeth others, lest they become weak." /

"My brother-in-law carves in wood. He could make it." /
"Build your houses high, lest the flood of men

floweth by." /
           "My daughter! In college but hates it.
Her chisel and hammer carve the blood of sin

"each day. She's made a one-tonner of Christ crushing Satan,
a three-hundred pounder of Lust sneaking in as—" /
"She done any of commies and all their hating?" /
The woman's grey eyes paused. "Why I believe she has!" /

"You say that she's in college. You have a picture?
Something from her high school yearbook would work." /
"My friend here," J Ed said, "is thinking of scripture.
Is she pure? Do no commies or sin within her heart lurk?" /

"A virgin pure. She hates to read. Two times failed
in English. Them professors say she writes things on the fly.
But she's a good girl, she don't lie. She's got brains in her pail.
The prophet John says, 'Lies bring on a sty in the eye.'

"You'd think they'd be glad she was so creative and smart." /
"That's just like those big brains. Each one rings up
some foreign plate. I'll ship them to Russia with heart." /
The mother sniffed. "It just makes them mad when she brings up

things they don't know." /
                        The judge too sniffed, "Is there a younger sis?" /
J Ed stirred. "Madam, he's just seeking knowledge." /
The judge rubbed his thighs when Momma nodded in Christian bliss.
"Does this younger sis who's not in college

have talent for sculpting?" /
                   "Roy, you know, my back yard's just filled
with handsome Greek statues, such pure and white
Adonises—" /
            Diogenes, having fulfilled
his pre-lunch search, which coughed its usual blight,

had strolled in to catch cool air. For one small second
he thought that Plato bounced in the voice of J Ed,
what with knowledge and handsome Greek lads. He reckoned
not, though. Both these two had already shred

his lantern's honesty meter by tossing it
headlong toward an Alabama trash-filled gutter. /
J Ed, meantime, pulled an index card, embossing it
with notes on the daughters of the patriotic mother.

He just hoped the Judge wouldn't throw a cog and balk
at a *female* Christian sculptor. Dress her in drag!
He'd once gone like such for a womanless wedding. The walk
he'd perfected! *Too hard to pull in B'ham slag.*

But all told, a Christian sculptor would be just grand.
Allay the Marxist guy who'd done that fountain in Five Points.
Hell's bells, I know Lenin's snout when it lands.
And that Bob fellow shares Semitic nasal joints. /

As J Ed mused, Dio rested his two-millennia legs.
He'd promised Doc Eddie he'd meet him here,
the Doc still gung ho over haints sharing full kegs
of illogic with living humans. 'Twas sheer

nonsense to conceive anything else, Dio knew.
Just take a gander at these shouting two. He'd grant them zeal;
that much he wouldn't deny. But zeal covered a slew
of itchy motives, motives zeal would never feel,

but which good ol' Doc's FMRI would reveal.
As Dio watched the two cavort he thought: Humans!
They *would* invent a machine to identify and seal
their fate, then ignore it, denying the true man.

Instead they'd wibble and wobble as they cobbled
out so-called strictly defined, strictly pure plans.
What truly moved them lurked deep hidden to hobble
their logic and mind-gears like clogging desert sand.

With a sigh, Dio strolled to the coffee emporium.
"Give me a tall one, the strongest you have,
make it iced, outside's hot as a Baptist exordium."
This marked the first coffee Dio'd ever had.

He needed caffeine to lift his flagging spirits.
Good thing pink Pluto wasn't around. He'd give bay,
and want a ham-smoked Dog Biscuit. Frill's will—Dio feared its
pursuing weight. He watched as J Ed gave sashay

across the floor. He watched the Judge watch a computer screen
where the First Five Furies hopped, flexing their bodies,
promoting free love education to angry screams
from listening patrons. Life, Dio fretted, stayed shoddy.

Vickie'd assured him that those five were virgins.
Won't stay that way long, he figured, even without
the schemes of Judge Bean. Sex—one more primal urging
all humans fought. Vickie, without a doubt,

to that hot fact gave note. /
                                          "Oh no," the barista cried,
serving Dio his first ever caffeine. He looked behind:
six patrons were fighting. It was enough to give the lie
to his lantern. Honesty? Just how could he ever find

that commodity up top, or down below, either one?
Doc Eddie walked in the door. Dio broke out a smile.
Wait! Look! Behold! Alonzo, the cop who'd shunned
his lantern for over a month with his bayou wiles,

stepped right beside the Doc. Dio gulped the caffeine.
It might set things a-flow. He bent down low
and nearly crept toward the cop, who stayed half lean,
half alert. *Cop the cop*. Though Dio's giggle sounded low,

it warned Alonzo. E'en with caffeine, Dio crept too slow.

Chapter Thirty-four: Hot Dog Rita and Homeless Lena

Hot Dog Rita goes bail for Homeless Lena and, on hearing rumors about Judge Roy Bean Too's monument plans, hopes for a hot dog franchise that will retire her to the coast.

When Hot Dog Rita missed her friend Homeless Lena
she sent out word amongst the 'Ham's kit cats.
She finally heard from one who sneaked between a
fleet of cop cars to sift through the jailed human rats.

Lena stuffed a note in that kitty's crimson collar:
Durp! I'm stuck in jail! Humans on Luna!
Well okay, Rita thought, I'll just give one holler
to Tony's Bonds.   The bail showed hefty, to the tune of

ten grand. *Say what the world*, Rita thought.
But Tony loved her dogs, and she loved his log,
so from behind bars Lena got wrought.
"Learned your lesson?" Rita asked. /
                                Lena, not one to flog

the moral of a story, just said, "Durp."
Though Rita preferred dogs to cats (was a pun
for which Dio would have given zipper, gladly, and shirt)
her fondness for Lena had overcome

misgivings. They were once more in biz.
Loud rumors had it that the Judge and his no-commie friend
would soon erect monuments grand to start a tiz,
to show the globe Alabama embraced the End of Ends,

to show Muslims they had no corner on righteous,
to show liberals and unbelievers the door,
to show Hollywood and Lady Gaga how mighteous
good Southern red-eye ham gravy can pour.

That's swell, thought Rita, my no-commie dogs
will make down payment on a condo in Fairhope,
will fatten Lena's kit cats, may make enough to jog
a franchise and buy me a twenty-foot boat.

My dogs, again, will make America bloat.

Chapter Thirty-five: A trip to Hades, a Pop Back Up Top

Diogenes travels back to Hades in hopes of procuring some type of sonar device for his wooden lantern that Joseph made. With such, he thinks, he'll be able to long-distance test Alonzo the mocha cop, whom Diogenes remains certain will prove to be the first honest man.

That even with caffeine he'd failed to lanternize the cop
sent Dio down once more to Hades, his brows dead knit.
Sure enough, Vulcan had risen to swear off wine's sop.
But D gave note that Hades made a bottle of red flit

behind Vulcan's back, even as he proudly swore,
"Nope. Never no more. You can test me with your lamp
if you don't believe." /
                          "The very reason I came ashore,"
D answered. "A prospect keeps building, but my tries stay damp.

"Can you maybe attach some Pythagorean chord
to work its music, like spheres from afar?"
Vulcan's brows turned frosty; he was shifting to Thor.
"Music's for wimps, unless from a kettle drum. Stupid stars

"a-twinkle put you Greeks in saccharine coma.
Hey, who the hell made that shitty wooden lamp?
No, let me guess . . . I smell a Jewish aroma.
Ol' Joe should stick to crutches, leave real amps

to me." The bottle of red roamed into Thor's sight.
He snorted, he swayed. As if alive, the bottle gave tilt.
Thor's tongue got wetted from his lip's delight.
Resolve melting, his spirit did also wilt.

The magic bottle bobbed and glistened.
Lord Hades purred, "A good red's gurgle gives smolder."
He popped the cork. "Music? Just you listen!" /
Thor lunged. When his fiery tongs caught Dio's shoulder,

Dio withheld a scream of pain. He'd not give Hades
the pleasure. "Guess I'll just upside flicker then.
Passed a guitar repair shop while marching with the ladies."
The Underworld Lord and Thor snickered when

Dio mentioned the fairer sex. Dio gave point
to their middles. "Wanna try doing without 'em?
One rumor about your tongs massaging his forked joint
would leave you both clutching waxed bananas, not hens."

Hades made motion, but D was quick. Topside did he spin.

Chapter Thirty-six: The Judge and J Ed Hire a Christian Sculptor(ess)

J Ed follows the Christian mother with the talented Christian sculpting daughter to the ladies room. Though tempted, he does not go therein, but relieves himself at a men's urinal, momentarily regretting his assistant Clyde Tolson. He then waylays the mother outside, where he and the Judge agree to interview her daughter for the first-ever Christian sculpting post.

J Ed followed the Christian mother to the john.
Almost, he went in. He valued ladies' toilets
for their private stalls. No never-need to let on
what tunes you fiddled there within. Public roil wets

one's privacy; it mars the capitalist way.
J Ed preferred each for each, not all for all.
Today though, in fear he'd miss what Mommy might say,
he rushed a urinal row, forsaking a quiet stall.

Not too shabby, he thought, spying his peeing neighbor.
But no one's weenie can match my Clyde's firecracker.
He heard a ding. The warning he'd planted to belay her
gave sound. He zipped and rushed out to track her.

"Madam, if I may . . . Your talented daughter . . .
might we talk with her? She's not no commie,
is she?" /
              "No thanks to my husband, that rotter!
He attends meetings nightly, he's a zombie!

"Swears by this book they read every durn day."
J Ed's eyes widened, taking in her stacked black hair.
Das Kapital? Good Heavens! The Reds have sway! /
"Makes it to step nine, then whiskey. It's not fair!"

Ah, the Big Blue Book and AA Anonymous.
Good weak folk, so that's okay. Keep it simple.
Twelve steps. Not complex like that Hieronymus
Bosch wart, a fellow traveller, a slimy pimple.

Was it possible to be a commie before commies
were dispatched? For certain. England had its Diggers;
and all those communes in New England's balmy
days. It only took Marx to pull the trigger.

"Weak, weak, weak," J Ed commiserated.
"You and your daughters, though, the strong hands we need.
Your oldest's sculpting talent has compensated
for sins of the father. Our vision, in her hands, will lead

"this vast and great commie-free land of ours to—" /
"Let America hate again?" the mother ventured. /
"Exactly. Can we meet her? She may hold the power to
once more get our vast and great land re-centered.

"And we can pay," he added slyly, viewing the dowdy
print dress that Momma wore. /
                                        Just then the Judge
walked up, his snakeskin boots so shiny. "Well howdy,
good ma'am." Too old, he thought, but her daughters' fudge

will taste much sweeter. "You're the lady with Christian
sculpting daughters. It sure would be fine and neat
if we could use their talents. Good Christians on mission
Could take America by its panties—" /
                                        "Its seat,"

J Ed corrected.
                    Momma was smitten.
Off the three drove, to interview her daughters . . .
In some Good Somewhere Book it's surely written,
"Like lambkins they would be led to slaughter."

If not, well, some fine poet pen it sure oughter.

Chapter Thirty-seven: Dio Visits a Stringed Instrument Repair Shop

Diogenes has escaped Hades' anger over his threat to spread rumor about Hades and Thor's sexual proclivities, and he has teleported back up top to stand before Burns Stringed Instrument Repair Shop. To his delight, Diogenes finds that the shop is nestled in a Greek enclave. It slowly dawns on him, however, that no one can see or hear him, for in sick jest Lord Hades has sent him up top without a body. He thus roams about as just one more confused haint, proving Doc Eddie's FMRI machine correct.

Ah Dio, do you measure truly for naught? For
two-thousand, four hundred and ninety-three years,
(Not to be a time stickler, but truth must be sought, or
to what might mortals cling? An orange guy with no beard?)

your lantern has passed its judgments fatal.
No honest man here, no honest woman there.
But wait! There's still that mocha-colored cop, playful
lovemate of V. Of honesty, doth he partake great share?

D'd left Hades and popped at Burns' Instrument Repair.
"Jason Burns, proprietor," its fine sign read.
A good Greek name, indicating fleece to share.
As Dio turned, his shoulder burned from movement of his head.

Some joker Hades proved, with that floating bottle of wine.
The blister from Thor's hot tongs would take months to heal.
*Well that's just fine, I can almost taste praise divine
that will turn mine when chords one honest man reveal.*

To the right of Burns' was a Greek wine and cheese shop.
Around the corner, a restaurant serving honey-soaked
baklava. Mystic, musical spheres surely would pop
themselves about. "Heigh-ho, Lantern!" D joked.

Pythagoras, surely you abide somewhere near!
D heard a banjo's twang. How ol' Hades did love
to play that and a fiddle! He'd pull out warm beer,
a fire he'd stoke (onto which listeners he'd shove).

Despite that rascally sound, Dio strode straight in.
A man sat plucking the banjo—on his knee,
by Zeus! From the photo out front, the man playing
was owner Jason, with a sharply cut black goatee.

Though such coif set Dio suspecting the Dark Lord,
torments below surely kept that one too busy to be
up here. Such a sidetrack he could hardly afford.
Recalling his goal—wily Lonzo—D began his plea:

"Excuse me, sir. I'd like you to attach a mystic chord
to my lantern. A minor key would work best.
In case I need it in a cavern." D snored
at his pun. The shop owner blinked, playing close to the vest,

D reckoned. "I can pay . . ." He hoped Hades hadn't slipped in
more drachma, claiming to forget. He checked his purse:
Great, just good ol' U.S. bucks had been flipped in.
"You see, I need a mystic chord in the very worst

"of ways. I've got to check for an honest man—
a curse, it's my lifetime task, I cannot help it.
Anyhow, there's this one mocha cop, and he's ran
off every time my lantern—its meter's self-lit

"to measure without fail . . ." /
                              The owner, Jason, blinked,
returned to his banjo. A catchy tune, but still . . .
"Say, I recognize that. Ol' Satan—who would think
he'd play a lick?—grinds it on fiddle, with a will."

Jason Burns stopped to tune up, then down a string—
had sounded fine to Dio, but musicians' ears,
who could deny them? "Say, guy, that's a mighty pretty thing
you made there. Think you could—" D stopped. Something was queer.

The owner once more blinked and missed a note or so.
"Say, can't you hear? My empathy to plucking in the zone,
but man, I need some help. This cop's ruining my show.
A mystic chord, methinks, would give him the jones."

A customer walked in. /
                              "You're here for the Taylor.
Fixed that crack just fine. They use a special seal,
had to take my time, else it would fail or
"give off buzz." /
                              "Paid three grand for it," the guy squealed.

"I collect 'em. Got twenty-three." /

"Wanna play it?"

"Is it in tune?" /

The owner blinked. /

At least it's not just me,
D thought. The guy clobbered a chord. "Don't know how to say it,
but thanks. Now I got twenty-four, not three."

He paid and left, hefting his guitar before him,
a badge. Jason sighed and went back to play.
"Excuse me," D called, "but my shedyule there's no ignorin'. . ."
He gave the Brit pronunciation, thinking that way

Jason the Argonaut might some attention pay.
It got not a blink. Wait, hadn't the collector bumped him
without reaction? No . . . Hades wouldn't play
that low a joke. D listened. The banjo tune stumped him.

His eyes narrowed when he recognized "The Devil's Trill."
If only I'd brought along Pluto, D thought.
No music fan, but he sniffs out bad jokes while lying still.
D inhaled. Grand Truth was what he sought.

The Argonaut Jason changed from "The Devil's Trill"
to "Ol' Scratch's Dream." Dio swung his lantern wildly.
He smelled goat cheese, he shouted in Greek, but got only still
that no-blink blink. "Help, I need. Bucks, I got." D spoke mildly,

though his patience ran tried. "Just one nice mystic chord.
I'm no musician, so it'll need to play with a strum.
Socratic: I know I don't know, unlike that bore
who just left." /

Jason played on and began to hum

"The Devil Went Down to Georgia." /

Dio screeched,
he waved his arms, he stomped his feet. "Devil
in Disguise," sounded out. /

"Sir Jason, I beseech.
Just stop and give a listen. I'm on the level."

Jason began to sing, "The Devil's Worst Sorrow."
Insight-filled, Dio's forehead sweated and glistened.
Invisible. He could yap here for twenty tomorrows
and Ol' Jason would not ever listen.

Dio made a grab for his peter, but stopped.
Lord Hades had tidily shut that down too.
His every protest seemed doomed to flop.
He flapped his arms until he damn near flew.

The Argonaut couldn't see or hear a thing. *A haint,*
that's what I am. "Hades, you bastard!" Dio flung his lamp,
which hit the owner's head. Jason didn't even faint,
but kept playing, though the throw unwrung D's lamp,

which broke in three pieces. Dio stared at the floor,
hardwood, oak he supposed. Ol' Joseph would be glad.
Vulcan, however, would do his best to ignore
that aspect. Dio picked up the pieces, sad

that he'd get no mystic chord. *Have to face the music,*
and it won't be bluegrass or any type of pretty,
it'll be Vulcan and Lord Hades, abusive.
It'll be gleeful, vengeful, and shitty.

Too bad. The Argonaut here plays swell. More's the pity.

Chapter Thirty-eight: Slam Sam Seduces Her Uncle

Sam Slam follows her plan to rejuvenate "Dynamite City" with her uncle's supply of dynamite that he uses in the mines. To procure it, she offers her body to her not so avuncular uncle, who suffers a heart attack in flagrante and dies.

Her uncle once claimed "some little Jap girl"
had given him the clap. Sam stared at his sweaty
fat red face, thinking she'd like to send him awhirl,
pop his bare white rump atop a bouncing betty.

Spread whale blubber here, spread it over there.
Instead, she let her crimson bra strap slip
enough to incite a grin; then she returned his stare.
"Remember our deal. You'll show me how to hook up and flip

"a dynamite switch." /
                              "You never said why you wanted—" /
"Let's just say I'm continuing what Granddaddy did." /
Her uncle smiled. "A real man. Kept them niggers disjointed.
After that church and them four girls we kept him hid

"for six years." /
                    A lie and Sam knew it. Who in hell would brag
about killing four kids? Her cracker uncle's who.
"Show me," she said. /
                              "Show me," he said. /
                                                      This could drag
forever, Sam thought. May as well give the old guy a screw . . .

All the while her uncle snorted, Sam saw sugarplum
headlines: "Cullman Man's Penis Exploded."
A little knowledge is a dangerous thing. Wasn't there some
blah-blah like that? She felt his pipe as it corroded

her twat. The end will justifit the means,
she thought. Uncle's TNT could disintegrate three hundred
self-righteous Southern Baptist pricks who roamed unclean
through streets. Males only, unless she blundered.

The new UAB football field would be the ticket.
Some frat boy penises full of beer and Jesus,
grabbing boobs, chasing pussy like rabbits in a thicket.
Women rule now! You dickheads better believe us.

Her uncle heaved, near heart attack; her plans she formed.
Those Muslim creeps want eighty-two virgins as reward
for jihad death. Sam grinned. Me too, for every dick I've scorned.
Her uncle's face: it really did look untoward.

She beat his chest. "Bastard! You died before I'd scored!"

Chapter Thirty-nine: Victoria and the Furies Get Sourced by Computers

Victoria is awoken by her computer's seemingly amiable ding. Its message makes her question her past life and its antics. Resolute, she awakens the Furies to continue their podcast tasks, while she surfs the Net to find a disturbing list that reminds her of something long past, but what, she can't quite finger.

On hearing her computer's ding, Vickie gets awakened.
"Dear friend," the message read, *"have you heard the latest?*
I've never been so sickened, so heart-broken, so shaken.
The Orange Guy is surely not making us the greatest!

Can you help? Donate now. Signed, Nancy Believe Me Mostly."
It seemed to V that her past-life's speaking tour
had run always positive. Or was that ghostly
prejudice? Exposing the Beecher preacher boor

had shown hard negative. And Mamma's blackmails here and there.
The means befit the ends? Maybe? Do they not?
She looked to Abby in sugarplum sleep, one shoulder bare,
awaiting loving touch. Would Dio's lamp swirl into shock

with her and the Furies? . . . She who hesitates . . .
Vickie clapped her hands to awake the Furies.
They scrambled about, podcasting to elevate
The Cause . . . but . . . their work . . . angry or cheery?

As V pondered all this she skimmed a site well-known,
though its Latin phrasing caught her off guard:

> *Index Verborum Prohibitorum*

Alone, that Latin seemed mal-said, hard-thrown.
She tugged a curl. Something about the phrase jarred.

But this was a good and liberal site, Lulu's List . . .
how could it hold wrong? She spied Abby directing
in one corner—and remembered her own first kiss:
it hadn't been pleasant. She'd spent weeks deflecting,

but then her father sold her, for "just five minutes,"
to an elder neighbor. "Do what he wants, we need money."
Well, much better for Abby. That, to finely spin it,
was the point. Spread not hate, but love's sweet honey.

That screen again: *Index Verborum Prohibitorum* . . .
Who else had published something like that?
But Lulu's Lists were pure! One couldn't ignore them.
To think bad of them would sting like that

sour poison the Orange Guy so glibly spread . . .
But still . . . who else had published something like this?
Would be too sad to think Lulu's List lay in the same bed
as close-minded, non-thinking conservatives remiss.

V looked back to the screen. Beneath the Latin
sat this translation: *Index of Forbidden Words*.
Forbid a word? Her journalist brain smelled a rat in
that. It sent her searching for Prilosec against gerds.

Taking two, she inspected this List of Forbidden Words:

> *Index Verborum Prohibitorum*
> *Never should these be said, not even in your head!*

> They all surround us, they're all about us.
> Nefarious they are, able to rout us.
> Take care we must, that they do not out us.
> Only the crassest and cruelest would use 'em.
> Use? That's hardly the word! Ab*use* 'em!
> Take care, my sweet and loving friend, to refuse 'em.

> The dreaded 'N' word floats its lard about.
> You know, of course, there's so much hard about
> that word. Beware, beware. Keep your guard about,
> even in quotes it should never be said.
> How painful e'en to write that 'N' instead.
> Perhaps . . . yes! The alphabet's 14th letter should be shed.

> That awful 'C' word. Can people really use it?
> And it's not just men! No, women strew it
> referring one to another! Sally, please chew it
> and swallow. Harsh appellation for anatomy so lovely, so pink.
> Mary, please stop before spitting it out. Janet, think!
> Yes, that third letter lies on exile's brink.

And further on . . . that awful 'F' bomb!
And yet the crass shout it with such aplomb.
Just hearing it said destroys our heart's glad song.
Take heed, gentlefolk dear, your tongue to keep clear.
Avoid those cursed four letters for an act so dear . . .
The alphabet's sixth letter must disappear, we fear.

The list, oh it does go on! "Spic," "Mick," "Frog," "Kike"
Three more letters gone. (*Frog* and *F Bomb* starting alike)
We want *all* political incorrects to take a hike!
And off-color jokes? Don't get us started!
"The rabbi, the priest, the preacher" should stay departed.
"The gay guy who walked in a bar?" Keep him uncharted.

If your jokes or words can make anyone sad,
delete 'em! Don't repeat 'em, e'en on the gad.
Thus cleansing our land will make the whole world glad.
And those reminders of yesteryear's evils?
We mean statues and flags, metaphorical boll weevils.
Historic cleansing works wonders to refresh the easel.

Tear 'em down, rip 'em up! No museum should hold 'em!
Those uniforms, those flags, don't even fold 'em!
Don't crate 'em, don't store 'em! Be emboldened!
That past slate should be cleansed, not remembered.
How celebrate spring, if we cling to December?
Oh dear heart, keep sweet, keep loving, keep tender!

Burn 'em, churn 'em, gouge 'em, destroy 'em!
Above all else, don't ever deploy 'em!
And shun, nay castigate, nay banish those who enjoy 'em!
This world, given a chance, could coast so pure.
It could roll, it could whirl, like a spinning top sure.
But only if you, dear heart, don't cast evil manure.

In brief, be correct, be aware, be political!
Don't let unthinking slimes hypocritical
draw you down the word-woe highway. Stay analytical!
Should you sense the onset of an evil trigger,
demand its speaker be silent until he/she figure
a civilized manner, and speak with less rigor.

Devise your own compact *Index Prohibitorum*!
Keep it handy for use. Don't ever score 'em.
Don't paint them on the walls of your lavatorum!

Vickie blinked at that last overblown word.
The author should have taken her own advice
and left that twelfth letter "L" dropped, unstirred.
Vickie then thought, *Am I being very nice?*

Her auburn curls all itched, as if covered with lice.

Chapter Forty: Facing the Music in Hades

Diogenes, angered that he'd been sent up to Burns Instrument Repair Shop as a bodiless haint, rushes down to Hades to complain, and also to get his lantern repaired from the angry toss he'd given it.

"A joke's a joke," Diogenes gave yell.
Lord Hades was banging away with a hammer,
but he did speak up at this intrusion in hell:
"Wouldn't be right to use musical glamour

"on that lantern you sway." He tucked his penis. "Pshaw,
we can't be using supernatural stuff above.
Just think of the precedent. It would appall."
Lord Hades gave nod to Joseph, whose gloves

looked bloodied. Joseph winced and held a stob.
Lord Hades raised his sledgehammer, "Ain't that right, ol' Joe?"
Ol' Joe gave quick nod. —Not smart, when you're on the job,
to give the grand Lord of chaos a negative go.

Lord Hades sighed; icicles tinkled from his mouth.
"That Thor's wine-drunk again. It'll have to be Joe
who re-rigs your lantern. I know it's hot down South
in the 'Ham, but try to hold your temper. Go slow.

"The good news is that Joe's picking up in metals.
Be a sport. Do let him have a shot at your lamp.
Hell, if it don't work, well a week's like a petal
against the near three millennia you've given tramp

"trying to find just one honest fellow. Oh I forgot,
you're now searching amongst the female types too.
How's that working for ya?" /
                                        Dio wished a rot
of pox on the Lord, but kept his mouth glued.

Complaining would only get him even more screwed.

Chapter Forty-one: Sic Semper

A fact arrives, a question gets asked, a poor moral gets given, to be followed by yet one more fact.

Slam Sam, she had a van.
She drove it down, toward Birmingham.
She'd packed it up, with dynamite tight.
She hit a bump, and blew out of sight.
Is there a moral to this too brief story?
Those who plan evil, they end up gory?
Surely you don't believe that rot.
Surely more earthly brains you've got.
Nonetheless, this stays true: Slam Sam had a van.
It and she blew up, a little north of Birmingham.

Chapter Forty-two: Doc Eddie Consults with Dio

Wherein the Doc, still in awe at his FMRI discovery, stands on a Birmingham street and asks for reassurance from Diogenes, that long-searching, long-suffering Greek. For every name the Doc brings up, Diogenes proclaims that his honesty meter judged the same with a final sputter.

"You mean to say—" Doc leaned to give Pluto a pat—
"you've never found even one?" /

                        "Spinoza was close,"
D said, "as was Buddha." D told of The Holy One at
the river Styx, pounding in anger for most

of three centuries, his reincarnation rage. /
"Well, what about Jesus, then?" the Doc asked. /
"Close again. But he clung to Mommy far past the age
you'd expect of any prophet. In fact, he basked

"in her perfume. Sage was then the rage. Not too sage,
get it?" /
       The doc made obligatory inhalation
at Dio's pun. Dio himself seemed to turn a page
inside his mind. "Spinoza, ah. Pure exasperation."

Dio tapped his forehead. "He kept something up here.
About . . . you know . . ." /
                       Doc leaned. "Life's meaning?" /
Dio blurted, "Let's talk of matters holding good cheer." /
"But surely you won't leave me without *some* gleaning!" /

"All right, here: Spinoza ground out lenses." Dio tapped those
on his nose. "He made these. But in that powdery room
of his—you know his synagogue made a great show
of cursing him both day and night until doom,

"willing that angel choirs flit about him thrashing
and torturing his misled ex-Jewish soul,
demanding he be exiled, friendless, stay mashing
his lenses in some nearby Holland-ish hole."

D shifted the aged lenses. " He fell in love, you know." /
"Is that why he failed your lantern's exam?" /
With a hearty chortle, D exclaimed, "Oh no!
I'd never hold that against any woman or man."

Dio took off his lenses and cleaned them. Pluto made moan.
"He glimpsed what wasn't human, the secret, forbidden word." /
"God's name?" /
            Dio spat. It sizzled in a no-parking zone.
"His dying breath, he gave it utter: 'Pshaw.' " /
                          "But that's absurd!" /

"Precisely." A bus's SPCA sign gave play
to "Save them all!" Pluto's docked tail wagged ovation.
"In brief, there you have the supreme why of the way."
As the bus's brakes squeaked, so did Doc in irritation.

He angrily voiced further ponders: Gandhi. Muhammad.
Those two surely deserved a tick from Dio's lamp.
But when for those august fine names the Doc had pled,
Diogenes gave his fist a squeeze, a steely clamp.

"Mahatma wore thick glasses and badmouthed blacks.
Muhammad spent inordinate time in a cave. Creepy.
When searching out perfection, one can't deny facts,
one can't simply start a fan club, rave, and go all weepy." /

"Abe Lincoln," Doc puffed in pride. "He freed the slaves;
he saved this great land." /
                    Dio just shook his head.
"You know he spent chilly by Willie, among cold graves.
What's more: to die at that poor comedy? He should have fled.

"He hardly could afford to watch at the Ford."
Dio smiled. He was getting a rhythm.
If V could stay here and screw, he could go pun on the boards.
They'd both avoid below's woes Lord Hades would give 'em. /

"Einstein!" Doc shouted in huff. "He fled the Nazis!
He gave us Relativity!" /
                   "Rebuttal lies within
that very word. Too coldsy, too hotsy.
Please, Albert, can you leave us one clear limn?" /

"Plato," Doc intoned, but seeing D's insipid laugh,
said, "Never mind. His drinking, all those boys."
The Doc kept still a moment before another pass,
his own honesty distracted by street noise.

This guy's lantern scale is showing way too strict.
With horns blaring, lights changing, carbon emitting,
no human can be expected to live sans some conflict.
Just standing on this corner sends my eyeballs flitting.

He narrowed those eyes. "Florence Nightingale,"
he whispered in dare. /
                          "She slept with a patient,
a major ethics flaw." /
                          "You're reaching beyond the pale." /
"That I cannot help. It's demanded by my station." /

"Vaccines! Edward Jenner! Dr. Jonas Salk!
The lives, the heartache they both did save!" /
"Jenner dinged those milkmaids until they balked.
Salk went on radio just so admirers might rave." /

Would all, Doc fretted, get shot down by this Greek,
a real tough hombre with his honesty meter?
"Mother Teresa!" Doc shouted with joy. "Her sallow cheeks,
her resolute eyes. She surely didn't teeter!" /

"*Au contraire*, her faith did waiver." /
                                          Doc shook
his head. "But she drove on through that to save
a hundred thousand or more! Just give one small look
at her work in Calcutta!" /
                            "There are plenty who naysay

"against her for not distributing birth control,
for not providing free junior college education." /
Doc's eyes slit toward Dio's lantern. An urge to bowl
it in fast-moving traffic struck. Pluto gave salvation,

for he nudged Doc's hand away. Was Dio's turn to inhale;
Please, not another trip to Hades. Vulcan or Joe,
it didn't matter. As long as Dark Lord ruled that swale—
he grimaced at a thought impossible. "You know,

he started, "the most honest one's a creep—" /
"The orange guy?" /
                    "Wasn't thinking of him, but yes, he'd do too.
Was thinking of our ruler Way Down Deep,
Lord Hades. There's never a doubt about what he will do:

"Something sick, something bad, something to get a laugh." /
"Sounds like Orange Guy to me." /
                              "But Orangey's a politician.
Automatic disqualifier. Their gaffs
are documented and well known, more rhetorician

"than honest. Lord Hades, though, he rules supreme.
He has no need to please, so he never gives bother." /
'The Orange Guy'd like that," Doc said. "Fulfill his dream." /
D swung his lantern at wobbling high heels, fodder

for failure's flicker. "A trans in drag," Dio said.
"How honest is that?" /
                              "I don't know. I'm confused . . ." /
"My point exact. We each give spill, as hope and dread
give wiggle." /
                   ". . . Confused so much I feel abused." /

"By your own thoughts?" /
                              "I guess." The Doc longed for his car
which held two bins of dark chocolate almond candy.
He felt sore in need of comfort food to tote him afar.
He felt sick, ill-tempered, foul-headed, and randy.

Pluto gave a nudge, with a bright red leash.
"You want us to take you for a walk? We're out already." /
"No, no," Dio corrected. "Pluto's a real peach.
It's we who should walk to dissolve this blue funk so heady.

"A little jog, you think? A stroll through the zoo?
The Botanical Gardens?" /
                              "We could visit Vulcan." /
D's eyes gave roll, but what the hey. One more visit accrued
to that hothead might work to heal this sulking.

"Sure, let's take the hike. Do us both a favor though,
and call him Thor. Under that aspect he stays drunk,
he twirls his moustache and creates a happy row
of thunder and lightning. Vulcan tosses hot metal chunks."

In nearby shadow, J. Ed wrote, *2 commie lunks*.

Chapter Forty-three: Hot Dog Rita and Homeless Lena

Having bailed Homeless Lena from jail Hot Dog Rita tells of her plan to follow Judge Bean and J. Ed to Montgomery and wherever after.

A dozen cats surrounded Homeless Lena.
Some rubbed, some purred, some yowled, some scratched, some peed.
"So what in the cat litter world could mean a
bail bond like you had? It cost a lot of cat feed." /

"Durp," Lena replied. /
                      "Well okay then. Here's the plan:
We follow those two idiot males around the state.
I hear they're erecting some Montgomery stand,
religious gobbeldy. The Lord provideth fate.

"With Jesus on our side we'll sell hot dogs a-plenty.
Retire me to the coast; feed all your cats in the Ham." /
"Humans on Luna." /
                      "Not me. A coastal sentry
is what I'll keep, thanks to this Jesus-commie scam.

"—And to you, of course. The finest shill in the land."

Chapter Forty-four: J Ed, Diogenes, Pluto, Doc Eddie, and a True Christian sculptress Meet on Red Mountain

The Judge makes harsh judgment of the elder Christian sculptress and forsakes her for her young sister. J Ed says his goodbyes and heads for Red Mountain and Vulcan, where he knows he will find Diogenes and Doc Eddie, both of whom he suspects of communist leanings. The elder sculpting daughter, Mary, inquires if J Ed will give her a ride there. He complies, and the two encounter Pluto, Diogenes, and Doc Eddie. Thereupon, Mary draws from her cornucopia purse to distribute food and promote temporal satisfaction; from her cornucopia tongue to promote temporal peace.

Judge Bean was interviewing the Christian sculptress;
the fifteen-year-old daughter, that is. He'd espied
a wrinkle on the elder, which signaled adulteress.
So he placed paws on the younger, trying to glide

the chisel near her breast. At this, J Ed voiced his good-bye.
The mother stayed, glad to have a judge so famous
take note of a daughter so young. But sis dwelt not so high,
and eyed the Judge as if he were squamous.

"I'm off to Vulcan," J Ed announced. /
                                    Sis's eyes
gave shine. "Can you carry me there?" /
                                    "I'm not that kind." /
"I mean give me a ride. Vulcan is the guy
who inspired me, you know. You'd have to be blind

"to not be impressed—although he was a pagan." /
J Ed agreed. In his new car they hopped. It had steel plates
a-plenty, ambush to stave. "Hey, don't mean to be ragin',
but your friend back there—my momma, she rates

"him good and Christian, but he paws my sis, and Mommy
always gets taken, since our sad dad's a drunk.
Just last month—" /
                    "Promise you this: he's no commie,"
J Ed interrupted. /
                    "I mean, who'd have thunk—

"Hey, what's a commie?" /
                    J Ed nearly capsized,
he braked so hard. This generation was ripe pickings
for platefuls of unrighteous Marxist lies.
Education was failing. The states should hand out lickings

to set matters right. That much kept on target
with Judge Bean Too. "Commies are rotten bad. They're Reds.
They want to sink democracy's boat and forget
what made this country great." /
                    "That's like Orange Guy says." /

J Ed was holding his judgment on Trump.
Though the guy never mentioned blasting Reds,
and though he chased women like that Kennedy skunk,
well still, that scowl of his: a grand old flag, 'On me don't tread.'

When nearly up the mountain, they passed two guys and a dog.
"Aw, look at pooch. We should stop and give it treats.
Jesus said, 'Be kind to others, even if they're hogs.'" /
"I never heard that." /
                    "Moms says it of Dads when he's three sheets

"into his booze. Come on, let's stop."
                    J Ed obliged.
"Hi! I'm Mary, like Jesus's mom. Can I pet
your doggie? I carry treats for creatures of ev'ry size.
It's like the Bible says, 'Be unto all as if a vet.'"

Then Mary pulled three treats from her purse: a Milk Bone,
an Oreo, a Fig Newton. "Oh, sorry. I'm so lame."
She offered J Ed a honeyed biscuit. " 'Give, don't loan,'
the Bible says. 'And I believe. It's a downright shame

"the hate some folks spread. For them I have honeyed biscuit.
It creates a small-while smile." She gave J Ed a wink.
" 'Help those who won't help themselves, and you'll nix it,'
Timothy wrote. And he's like heaven's missing link."

The oldest guy shook a weird lamp, trying to affix it
upon her e'en as he chewed the fig. She skipped, one heart blink,
before he could focus its locus. /
                    The tricks it
takes, D griped. As Mary danced off, her hand did sink

within her purse to find one more doggie treat. /

Another?

Dio grieved. *This newly nimble generation*
will cause my downfall. How be accepted as brother
to great god Hades if I relay no information?

Doc Eddie, chewing the Oreo, intervened.
"You ever had an FMRI brain scan?" /
" 'Trust nor science nor what you read.' The epistles stay lean.
Why don't we walk on up? I want to see the iron man."

They left the car to take a stroll, Pluto giving lead.
Sweet Mary unhooked Pluto's bright red leash.
"The Bible says, 'The rules of man give heed,
but in your heart, holdeth only God to please.' "

She pointed at a sign about animals in the park,
then pulled a can of spray paint from her purse,
replacing *on a leash* with *kept free*. "Much less dark,"
she said with flourish. "People, they always think the worst

"of dogs and cats and birds. But Noah in his ark
saved them all—even snakes." To J Ed she handed
another honeyed biscuit. Chewing, he dropped a note card,
not seeming to care. Dio set his lantern down to stand

and give—was that a yoga stretch? Doc Eddie, he
eyed Mary's purse even as she pulled out a pad
and sketched a sketch. How spacious could it truly be?
He slyly prod: "A coffee shop atop would make me glad." /

" 'Drink with thine enemies to make them friends.'
The great Apostle said that. Look in my purse.
A battery powered Keurig, though only nine blends
of coffee would fit. Bottled water, I keep for a lurch."

Mary kept sketching. "From this I'll chisel a one-tonner
and call it 'Good Friends.' There's more biscuits with honey;
please pass one to J Ed. If he sours, would make a bummer." /
And thus, all ate, to keep matters light, to keep them sunny.

The three ravens returned and cocked their heads in wonder.
Below, was it truly the same place, same folk?
Where once did wallow hate, where once did peal out thunder?
They watched one tilt his head to drink. *Give us from your poke,*

the ravens thought. /
        " 'Tarry not,' sayeth John,
'The Lord hath work to be yet done.' " /
                "These scriptures,"
asked J Ed. "Where is it you get them from?" /
"*When I use a verse*, to give you the true picture,

"*it means just what I choose it to mean—*
neither more nor less." /
        "Just like on Sand Mountain,"
Doc Eddie said. /
      "Beg pardon?" /
           "My home, where snakes seem
to confirm one's faith. At least, that's wisdom's fountain

"up there. Most Christians don't—" /
           "Agree," interrupted J Ed. /
"Of course not," said Diogenes. "That's part of *their* faith,
to not agree, I mean." Pluto wagged his tail to be fed
one more Dog Bone. /
        "In hunger the soul doth stay,"

proclaimed Mary. "That's why I like to feed for free.
Did you know that stomachs control the souls?" /
"More scripture?" asked Dio. He edged forward to see
if his lantern could close in enough to take its poll. /

"Oh no, sometimes we must deliberate ourselves,
to show free will. 'Trust the Lord to give you succor.' "
Cookies, biscuits, and bones arose from her purse's shelf.
" 'Keep thine stomach full to defend as buffer

" 'from Satan's ways.' —sweet Matthew, I think." /
           They stared
at Vulcan's undersides. "In truth, he's much more wobbly,"
Dio tattled. "A winehead, he never can fare
assured past mid-afternoon." /
        "Drink is probably

"Satan's blood. Honeyed biscuits are angel's brows."
Mary stowed her sketch and pulled out makings
for jam and tea. /
      "What I marvel, is just how
that purse can hold so many wonders without breaking,"

J Ed offered. "It would make my nieces proud." /
"There is a bit of magic going around," said Doc Eddie,
thinking of his car. Diogenes stayed quietly loud
and tapped his lantern, getting it primed and ready.

This Mary just might be the one. Already, he could taste
the golden goose Hades had promised to roast.
This young woman would prove his life was not a waste,
when her honesty gave his lamp a golden toast.

His hands did tingle, his heart did skip an earthly beat.
A transported rock star, he shook and shivered.
This once he would be certain, he would be fleet.
While Mary smiled, the others eyed Dio's quivers.

Pluto dropped his Milk Bone, Doc Eddie raised his hand,
J Ed, he felt unnatural and forsook his trademark scowl.
All three did scramble to stay Dio's lantern on its stand.
Mary, perceiving something amiss, pulled a beach towel

from her purse. " 'Cover the ungainly, lest it mar a child,'"
she said. "Now that's sweet Matthew for certain." /

                                                         Dio gave yelp
as Donald Duck in cotton draped his lamp. The three stood mild.
"Would not do—" Doc Eddie spoke for the group— "to squelch

"a day so lovely. Keep your lantern's test for some other." /
" 'Rush not to judge, lest ye receive no fudge.'
That one's mine. Don't think fudge had been discovered
in Jesus' time." /

                              Taking tea under Vulcan, none begrudged.

Even Dio calmed and sipped, consenting not to budge.

Chapter Forty-five: The Judge and J Ed Visit CEOs A-plenty

The judge is frustrated in his designs on the younger sculptress by a drunken dad who wants to share a drink with the famous judge. Mary's honeyed biscuits pass through J Ed, leaving him once more pursuing commies. This leaves the judge and J Ed meeting with five oil executives, who plan a new and larger Horizon off Alabama's coast. In turn, the judge and J Ed explain their plan to erect a granite monument in Montgomery. In joyous confab, they agree to support one another. Together, they celebrate.

When the fifteen-year-old had stressed that *No means no*,
the judge caressed her cheek, her shoulder, her breast.
He was edging toward her cleft when who should show
but drunken Pops, who did his very best

to goad the judge, whom TV had broadcast wide,
to share a drink *mano a mano*, eye to eye.
This was the first favor Dadkins, on his side,
had done daughter for fifteen years. And he hadn't tried.

So the judge had fled converted, not to a god,
but to frustration and anger. J Ed also
underwent a sea-change: as Mary's biscuits trod
from his intestines, commies once more lit his show.

Not one day later, the two arranged a meeting
with five off-shore oil execs guaranteeing no spills.
The judge offered up good prayers and Christian greeting,
the execs nodded their nods; J Ed revealed their will:

The Granite Grant to save God and mommy,
get rid of commies. /
             "In Montgomery goes the first,"
one exec said. "Our capitol must stay free of commies." /
"They always hinder progress. They think the worst

"of our endeavors." /
             "Was oil that made America great." /
"Just one more well, a bit larger than Horizon." /
"Do you think your granite might carry a brass plate
mentioning our gift?" /
             "It might be enterprising

contacting Crowds on Demand. Good bang for the bucks;
they make a great swell," another inserted. /
"No need at all, we have true believers who give no truck
to opposition. /
          "Be nice if they converted

"those liberal commies who worship the environment." /
"Who worry hard-working men who simply want
to feed their god-fearing families and save for retirement." /
"Who think technology and oil will somehow haunt

"our tomorrows." /
                "Who cannot see what a small price
a teensy spill is to pay." /
                    "That oil will guarantee our future." /
"All in all, gents, we think your monument quite nice." /
"And we," Judge Bean replied, "see your new well as a suture

"for the ills besetting our great state and land." /
The five execs stood in salute: "Promote God and Mommy!"
The judge shook bullets in his revolver, high in his hand.
J Ed's jowls slathered, "And rid our land of commies!"

All seven felt they'd marked the room with their little tommies.

Chapter Forty-six: Victoria and the Furies Visit CEOs A-plenty

Before a meeting, Victoria relates to Abby how she brought her son back from death with the succor and love of her full breasts. Abby listens and forces a smile at the unbelievable news. Five CEOs from California's Silicon Valley arrive to meet with Victoria, Abby, and all the Furies. In joyous confab, they agree to support one another. Together, they celebrate.

" 'Permit his death I'll not!' I gave this shrill shout
upon learning that my son had died two hours before.
I unclasped my bodice and pushed my bosom out,
to suckle my son for seven hours full sure.

"And then, like Lazarus, he arose." Victoria explained
this to Abby, who listened half in fright.
"I never felt so exuberant, yet so drained
when his little skin began to sweat as I held him tight.

"*Never* will I lose a son or daughter. Death's afraid
to stare me in these eyes." /

                           Abby shifted in her chair.
She smiled a smile, not reflexive but made.
Was timed quite well, for five visitors showed up there.

These CEOs had flown from Silicon Valley
to offer parlay with Victoria and her crew.
Thus Abby: "The future lies in a rally
of forward-thinking progressives who know the true

"value of love and inclusive acceptance." /
One CEO spoke, "Computech will make us great." /
Another: "Our government must offer an injection
of new research." /

                     "Indeed, tax breaks must not abate." /

"Binary code is so much more than binary." /
"It opens the spirit, it boggles the brain." /
"Inclusive, you say? Yes, that forms its primary
goal. To expand."

                    "To grow thought like flowers in rain."

"Information's flow will create jobs." /
                          "Will work wonders." /
"Our tiny microchips stand like the shoulders of giants." /

"The future, I predict, will applaud our thunder." /
"Yes, ladies, with your open love we are compliant." /

"The time for trolley cars is gone." /
                              "Tele-transport!" /
"Time-travel!" /
              "Who knows where microchips will lead?" /
"Together in open love we'll pool our greatest source,
the human brain!" /
                    "Ladies, your idea is great. We need

to contact Crowds on Demand. Good bang for the buck;
they make a great swell," one last exec inserted. /
"No need at all, we have true believers who give no truck
to opposition." /
                  "Be nice if they converted

"the ignorant and misinformed, the hungry and lame
to forward thinking, intelligent programs,"
one exec said. /
                  "We see your work as a binary flame,"
the five glow-praised in unison to those mams.

"And we," V replied, "see your work as a suture
for the ills besetting our great state and land."
The five CEOs stood to salute, "To the future!"
The dancing Furies, they had no need to stand.

"Ah la," all shouted in communal caritas, "How grand!"

Chapter Forty-seven: If It Plays in Peoria . . .

Nearly a year has passed. All the CEO funds have come to fruition. The Judge and J Ed are in Montgomery for the unveiling of the first of the Granite Grants, huge statues meant to instill faith's fear through Alabama. Victoria, her Furies, Diogenes, Doc Eddie, Pluto, and Alonzo have traveled to the capitol in protest. And of course Rita is selling her hot dogs while Lena is acting the nefarious shill. Crowds on both sides have gathered. Matters are going smoothly enough when Diogenes spies Lord Hades, who's evidently beamed atop, disguised as a high school tuba player. Diogenes rushes to warn Victoria about the chaos that is sure to follow this, the Dark Lord's visit.

Peoria? Montgomery plays close. The Judge and J Ed
arranged for three country bands—J Ed did mention
Benny Goodman, at which the Judge shook his head.
And then, procuring paramilitary as henchmen,

all dressed in white robes, not for the Klan, but Jesus' sake,
they felt safe from Muslim intervention, and so
invited five high school bands. A big break
came with the sun, which sent a late September glow.

Not quite a year had passed since those fruitful meetings.
The fifteen-year-old had sculpted her installation:
a bearded man, commandments in right hand—and for bleating
bum doubters, a .45 in his left. Inhalations

a-plenty would stir from that, to cure their woeful doubts.
The sculptress, oh she was proud. Her momma gave rub
to her belly. Her sis had given long, hardy shout,
" 'Beware, be constant, keep thine garden from slugs!'

"Please mark that verse from Mark and shun the old guy's parts!"
Unheeded, though, Mary's words had gone. Young sis gave glow
as she sat by her installation. The Judge's arts—
and money—would surely prevent a paternity row.

The Judge, he placed one hand on her bare shoulder,
his other did give backward roam to her young friend,
who stood beside what she called, "The Holy Boulder."
Five digits made judgely visits, he wished he could use ten.

A firecracker went off. Everyone danced and laughed.
The Furies and Victoria had also hired three bands:
mariachi, jazz, and gospel—the latter a shaft
at the Judge, they hoped, for he took an Old Testament stand

and left Jesus beneath some pew. They too enrolled
five high school bands. The local ambulance service,
as bonus, sent emergency vehicles to patrol.
Five arms-makers hoped to keep folks secure, not nervous.

Five auto manufacturers did show.
Five fast food chains provided samples of their fare.
Five banks, their young sales execs all a-glow,
did offer instant credit, interest at minimum bare.

Five used car dealerships flew balloons and pennants.
Five health spas did massage various glands.
Of churches, five times five times five advised penance.
Five talk show hosts "stood firm by their stands."

Five Silicon Valley start-ups displayed their wares.
The five oil CEOs rode in five Mercedes,
The five Silicon Valley guys that act did share.
From ten shiny cars, ten gave wave. Chaos—Hades—

had he taken holiday? This thought made Dio gasp:
it surely was not up here that mad Lord would come.
Another firecracker. Everyone danced and laughed.
Dio swung his lantern, Doc Eddie, being not outdone

gave crackle to his portable FMRI.
In sequence both made tests. Amongst all this, Homeless
Lena handed tainted hot dogs out on the sly.
A troupe of mangy cats followed, *their* mouths foamless.

Hot Dog Rita, envisioning a condo on the coast,
gave pipe in her throat: "No-commie dogs here! Red hot!"
Of five separate vending trucks, she now could boast.
At her rumble, J Ed fretted. Was this somehow a plot?

With each red yelp that Rita made, J Ed bethought
his files' divides: *Summary Memoranda, Obscene File,
Confidential File,* and the very best he'd ever wrought:
the *Do Not File File.* He scribbled a note card and smiled.

Doc saw and neared. *What truths might this nut bring to view?
Will my FMRI machine blister amazed?
Poor Terri Schiavo's brain had scanned all white, no blue;
will this one's dazzle out a Technicolor haze?*

Doc wondered how he could coax J Ed's head within:
Might he claim the box a "Brainwash wash-away wash"?
Might he claim he'd found nudies of Tolson giving spin
to his Tommy? But J Ed's jowls would scorn such bosh.

No time! Ye Olde South Capitol sat before:
was pearly, was clean, was pure, simple, and white.
From opposite directions, the marchers gave bore
to shouts and cheers. Who could believe this noisy sight?

A half block away, V and Lonz stood side by side.
They smiled, they fretted—was that type of day.
Beside them, Pluto yipped, he growled—his own bumpy ride.
All in all, better to be a lily at field in play.

Horns tooted, sirens sounded, drums beat, tubas burped.
Dio paused mid-swing. *A wonder Hades doesn't rumble
that fat thing.* He watched a row of high-schoolers work
their cheeks. His eyeballs gave lurch. *Mount Parnassus give tumble!*

That nearest high-schooler had winked. D had no doubt:
the underworld Lord had hopped a beam-me machine
to pop above. D panicked. *Find V before the rout!*
He twisted, he turned, and though he stayed lean

his lantern got bumped. That jowly guy with those note cards!
"He's here!" Dio shouted. /
                          "Who? Lenin? Kennedy? Marx?" /
"No, damn it! Great Lord Hades! His tidal wave will retard
what little peace remains!" /
                            "At least no commies on his part,"

J Ed replied, hastily scratching more notes on his cards. /
"I've got to find Vickie, warn her!" /
                                      "She's miscegenating
with that black cop. To give 'em guns . . . times must be hard."
Dio's lantern again flickered: there came no debating:

no honesty here. This guy'd sell anyone but his mum—
and maybe Clyde Tolson—to promote his commie show.
The Doc's machine would scan him all red. What a plum
of a pun, D thought. But no one to hear—that's how it goes.

A firecracker popped. Everyone danced and laughed—
Dio turned from J Ed to spy a tall mocha head.
As he rushed toward it and Vickie, he felt a hot draft.
A lone tuba burped in the firecracker's stead.

That solitary, ridiculous sound filled Dio with dread.

Chapter Penultimate: As Fate Would Have It

The time for the unveiling of the first Granite Grant has come. The judge is standing beside his teenage sculptress, who will pull the golden cord and reveal the statue of a bearded god who holds the Ten Commandment tablets and a pistol. At its unveiling, the crowd gasps, some with delight, some with horror. Lassoes appear, and a tug-of-war ensues, with horrific results.

The tired old chants had started ten minutes before.
Each side grew raucous in promoting Truth Divine:
"Let America hate again." /
                              "Make fug, not war."
Lone tuba burps prompted them, bumping everyone's spine.

A red and white and blue crisp sheet lay draped
upon the statue, looming thirty feet high.
The Judge had christened it "None Can Escape."
The sculptress, Mary's sister, stood nearby,

a golden cord in hand, all set to tug and reveal
this newest vision, for this greatest land.
'Those there are," Judge Bean Too gave shout, "who hold God's laws unreal.
For them, He clasps an iron brand in his stern hand."

Judge Bean gave pause to note four girls at play
beneath his speaker's stand. Two were black, two white.
His lips gave twist. Would such impure acts lead the way
to lesbian miscegenation? Would foul weddings blight

this greatest land? "I must repeat: His judging hand
keeps strong. Good friends, our God holds love, but He stays stern
against those who falter." A showman, the judge reached for grand,
and nodded for the gold cord's tug. "Abide and learn,"

the Judge gave said. The patriotic sheet, it caught,
as it slipped, on the tip of the statue's .45.
The kindly Judge did help as the sculptress sought
to disentangle the red, blue, and white. "It thrives!"

the Judge gave shout as the sheet at last fell away.
A bearded man's heavy brows shown down on them all,
his right hand held Commandments Ten. He seemed to sway;
that mighty .45—would it prevent his fall?

"Thirty feet, all of it righteous!" the Judge screamed out.
"Yes." /
     "No." /
          "Yes." /
              "No." /
                   "Yes." /
                        "No." /
                              "Yes." /
                                    "No." /
                                        "Yes."

Did a burping tuba signal the coming rout?
However it came, lassoes were hurled from the west.

"Down with the vile thing!" was given shout as if to bust.
Then other lassoes were hurled from the east.
"Stay up it must! It's God's righteous hand, in which we trust!"
Back and forth, the giant statue teetered, though the least

advantage to one side, soon gave way to the other.
Newton's Third Law of Squiggle had held so far this day:
for each action, an opposite reaction did hover.
But entropy always plays: so very many more ways

the statue could lie flat than stand, so many more gashes
its .45 could rend in warm flesh than in air tepid.
So very clear it showed: something must give as the clashes
increased, and so very clear *that* something would be vapid.

Alonzo stood no more than forty feet away
when he saw it coming. The four girls had stayed
under the speaker's stand, which had also begun to sway.
As the statue at last did topple, as it did betray

not only Newton's Third Law, but any good intent,
Alonzo ran for those girls. As reward, the barrel
of the .45 his shoulder gashed. The air got rent
with the dying girls' screams as their marrow

conjoined in final miscegenation.
A distant firecracker blew. No one laughed, no one danced.
The crowd turned quiet at this fireless conflagration.
Moral? In mob rule, nothing bad gets left to chance.

A lone high school tuba player began to huff and prance.

Chapter Ultimate: A Drizzly Day

Devastated by the death of the four girls, the six retreat to Alonzo's apartment, where they make great moan. Diogenes threatens to lock his lantern in a walnut box, forsaking his search forever. There comes no protest from the others until Doc Eddie breaks the dismal spell by fetching Mary, who'd spread peace so well on Red Mountain amongst him, Diogenes, and J Ed Hoover. Mary of course hands out food and quotations throughout the night.

It was a drizzly day in the 'Ham.
They'd gathered at Alonzo's, but even yoga sitting
before the BVM could not undo the sham
encountered back in Cap City. Forgetting

that scene, impossible seemed. And so it was:
images of those four dead girls floated
in, then out like neon bad dreams, sending bad buzz.
Glumly the six sat, on and on. 'Twas V who first noted

Diogenes unloading steel locks from his pocket.
He placed each on the floor, near a walnut box.
"Where'd you get all those? Sneak to Hell in a beam-me rocket?" /
"Indeed no. I bought these items at Goodwill, though a pox

"rests hard on that foul name. Is none, was never, never will.
Quadruple locks shall hide this foolish lantern—forever.
Hades and his golden-goose-roast's poison pill
have becked their last false beck. This lantern and me are severed.

"These keys I'll drop deep in the River Styx.
Like Buddha I'll be. I'll throw off a piss
tantrum. My focus will click eternal on this:
four innocent girls and the lives they missed.

"Four dead girls. What grades were they in?
Did they play piano or sing? Squabble with their brothers?
Were they old enough to charm boyfriends?
Did they bake cakes with their mothers?"

Pluto's red tail was far too short to slide between his legs,
yet it seemed to lower, degree by ruddy degree.
Lonz on his tattered velvet couch half laid, to stare at dregs
of week-old Viennee weenies. Abby clutched her knees

to sigh so ragged it might have loosed a rattle of death:
"You can't mean you're forsaking your lantern for good." /
In reply Diogenes shrieked, "Evil leaves good no breath!
Those girls, innocent lambs, snatched before they'd withstood

"one dozen years of worldly woe." /
                                            "We *all* committed sin,"
Victoria said. "There's no *them*, no *they*. All of us tugged
those ropes in pride, unwilling to listen, much less give in.
We hated immensely, when we should have loved." /

"At least shoulda gived one tiny hug," Lonz quietly said.
Victoria bowed her head in slow cold nod.
Lonz's shoulder stayed bowed 'neath sterile medical pads;
this he accepted: never more would it serve as rod

for finding evil. 'Now on, he was just one more dumb cop.
He'd tried and tried, but felt no telltale quiver, no burn.
He turned to Pluto, V, Eddie, Dio, Abby: "A flop,"
he cried. "My arm's forsook its will to discern.

"My grand-mere's gift be lost." /
                                            'This plays worse than the Tombs,"
V said. "At least there no one died." /
                                            "At least in Hades
"we all expect the worst," D moaned. /
                                            "Barely out of the wombs,"
V continued, "they'll never grow to be ladies." /

Young Abby replied, "What's the use? Neither will I."
All six reclined, imbibing their morose decline.
Lonz's curtains stayed wide; outside on the balcony high,
where love had once been witnessed, a bleak sun gave shine

to move elliptical. A traffic light did change,
a horn gave toot, then blared. Three ravens spiraled down,
but just yards from tumbling into a suicidal, strange
black clump, they flipped, gave frolic like clowns.

All inside saw what half of their flight looked worst,
all ventured to draw no conclusion anew;
all felt that life would soon inflate and burst;
all dropped in bottomless shafts, pinned there by screws.

Abby thought she would just say yes to drugs.
Alonzo thought he'd dump Grandmere's voodoo.
V regretted her British manse and all its pretty rugs.
Dio worried his zipper. Was there anyone who knew

how to untangle the damnable thing?
Pluto thought back to when he frolicked as a pup.
Doc Eddie wondered if his FMRI could sling
his brain off—Wait! Those ravens! All three were rising up!

Doc Eddie himself rose to calmly state, "This, must we stop.
No one leave. Pluto, keep guard. Dio, don't dare pry
that cabinet door. In ten Mississipps, back I'll pop." /
"Oh Doc, we know how well you mean, but not FMRI." /

"No Vickie, not that, a wonder immensely better.
Pluto, your task. It might take 600 Mississippi's."
Pluto gave whine, but obeyed to the letter.
He crouched before the walnut cabinet in a jiffy.

Doc Eddie glanced back from Alonzo's door: the sight
he saw played woeful at best. Listless listlessness
around the room squirm-snaked dark plague, vile blight.
He hustled out, hopeful to set such matters to rest.

Dio fidgeted at his locks, but Pluto stayed firm.
Alonzo popped his shoulder, but heard no voodoo word.
Vickie planned one last visit to her burial berm.
They heard Doc Eddie's car start, but not a one stirred.

Abby was a counter. She began to mark the seconds;
reaching 400 she saw the front door re-opening.
In hopped sweet Mary. " 'Never should you reckon
while sitting at the table!' " Mary then began groping

her purse to toss them cherry cupcakes a-plenty.
"That was Matthew, by the way, to the money changers.
He went on, 'There'll be time enough to shent thee,
when the dealing's done.' Eat, eat, don't be strangers!"

Mary pulled a genuine Trump Steak from her purse,
to toss to Pluto. Doc Eddie grinned: was from his car.
"Low carb diet? I've got fried chicken. Hey, is there a hearse
outside and waiting? I've got eight sealed jars

of scuppernong jelly, five of blackberry jam.
Cheer up: 'It's not over until the fat angel rings
her trumpet out.' That's from the tall man with the plan,
ol' John on Patmos. So eat, jump, and sing.

"Hey! There's happier faces on a Clabber Girl Tin.
Rise up! My sister broke her arm in the platform's fall.
Those girls are dead. 'Satan sends detours! Don't slip in.'
Focus!—Using Siri to plan road trips would have helped Paul.

" 'If your coach is a pumpkin, why then, bake pie.'
The Puritans misquoted Luke. What he really said
was, 'Serve brambles and thistles for lunch if weeds grow too high.'
I mean, you all, 'Give thanks! You're still alive, not dead!'

"I'd offer honeyed biscuits, but the ol' commie chaser
himself ate my last." Pluto nudged the steak, then chewed.
Mary noted the empty can of Weenies and placed her
hand in reverence thereon. "Don't mean to be rude,

"but, say, do you have any more of those?
'Taste near, taste far, no taste tastes better than Viennee.'
She held an Oreo before Alonzo's nose. /
"Got three cans left," he said. /
                                    "Trade. Just one of Weenies,

"though. 'Whether thou doth drink or chew, stay slow.'
That may have been Elvis's mom, I admit.
The one about tasting is my very own, although—
Elvis and his Cadillacs sure make a close fit.

"Baby, it's just them he was dreamin' of.
Jesus said, 'Render unto Ford what is Ford's,
But give unto GM your hot steamin' love.' "
Thus Mary quoted through the night. Her quotes and food restored

a spark to all. At last Alonzo broke out his rum.
"We got to gives the first taste to good Saint Joe."
He poured a thimble over the statue and made low hum. /
"So *that's* why his work sometimes takes a shoddy glow,"

D said. "Sure wish we had ouzo or retsina,"
he added. /
    "Be back in five Mississips."
Doc Eddie jumped and ran on out. /
        "What's the dif between a
magic purse and a magic car?" Abby asked, giving flip

to her skirt as Vickie had shown. This did indeed
catch every male eye. /
        " 'Question not the gifts of grace.'
Paul, right after lightning struck, and on the road he peed."
Mary giggled. Had the rum begun its neuron race?

Doc Eddie burst back in, two bottles in his hands.
"One each," he beamed. "In the back seat of my car." /
Dio's mouth watered for a taste of Greece, but he made stand:
"It's Lonzo's home; he should get first sip from those jars." /

"Oh la, these juices weird, brewed in some cypress bayou,"
Lonz offered on sampling both. "But they raise us from this funk."
He passed the jars around. That old bird, time, it flew.
—Could this be right? What the Union of Poets says is true?

Other than pimples, do they really have something to bust?
Could their non-rhymes, their whines, their flaccid verse
really offer humanity something it might trust?
Or are their poems just one more slow-moving hearse?

And dawn—was it outside breaking, or was it just false?
" 'The darkest hour comes just before total fuck.' "
Mary clasped her hand over her mouth and spun a waltz.
"That one's from Satan," she said, "who wants us to run amuck.

"My daddy can't hold his liquor and neither can I.
But slurring or weaving, my counter-message stays true.
Don't trust Satan, keep your belief straight and high.
'A fish in water'—oh I forget—'hath no need of shoes!'

"That's Peter, the fisher of men. He's saying, Take a stand.
You've got to trust in what you're given. But then,
'I dreamed I was butter, who dreamed it was a man.
It churned and churned until it grew legs to spin.' "

At that, Mary gave five blinks. "Not too certain
what that one means. Inscrutable and Chinese.
'When the sun starts setting in your land, don't keep hurtin'.
Head west to reach new east; pilgrim, bend those knees!'

"You know, that one must be some latter-day-saint.
Ol' Joe Smith was a fruitcake, all right, but he had
spirit to tote those plates of gold. He wouldn't faint.
Pick up and trek out west—that's tough, that's rad."

Diogenes, listening, started fiddling with his lamp.
When he struck a Lucifer to give it light,
Doc Eddie ran. "Thought you and lamp had decamped,"
he shouted, giving wave behind, of which Vickie caught sight.

She hustled Mary and Lonz into a small back room,
while Abby yanked wide the apartment's door.
"That girl," Dio panted. "She'll play just the right tune
on my lamp. Her and that mocha cop. I implore

you all to hold them tight. Just two more lamp waves
will tell. Oh, what a finish! I can taste golden goose
served up with that Mary's blackberry jam. The raves
I'll get from Hades and the gods when I toss a noose

around not one but two honest lambs. Male and female,
can you beat it? The gods will stop snickering how I'm blind.
Hey! Where'd they go? Where'd they run?" /
                                                "Off. But they left a trail
of Oreo crumbs," Abby said, "following behind."

With a whoosh, out Dio, Pluto, and lantern did rush.
Onto the balcony, the five remaining made race.
Seeing lantern glow below, Mary gave bright blush
as Dio cried, "I'll find one yet!" and Pluto howled a-pace.

" '*Sic semper pyrus.*' Vulcan. It means, *Keep the faith.*"

Envoi, from book to author

Your drasty rhyming sings out not one dead dog's turd.
It piles up higher, skanky word on skanky word.
If I were Chaucer's host, I'd pop you in your nose.
From this time on, Bud, you had better write plain prose.

ALSO BY JOE TAYLOR

STORIES

Ghostly Demarcations
The World's Thinnest Fat Man
Some Heroes, Some Heroines, Some Others
Masques for the Fields of Time

NOVELS

The Theoretics of Love
Pineapple: A Comic Novel in Verse
Oldcat & Ms. Puss: A Book of Days for You and Me
Let There Be Lite: How I Came to Know and Love Gödel's Incompleteness Theorem